The Forest Ranger's Rescue

Leigh Bale

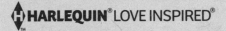

HARLEQUIN® LOVE INSPIRED®

Recycling programs
for this product may
not exist in your area.

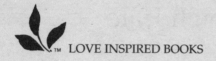

LOVE INSPIRED BOOKS

ISBN-13: 978-0-373-81824-2

The Forest Ranger's Rescue

www.Harlequin.com

Printed in U.S.A.

I wait for the Lord, my soul waits,
and in His word I put my hope.
—*Psalms* 130:5

This book is dedicated to the personnel of our US Forest Service, for their tireless work in conserving our national resources for the future.

And many thanks to Jill Jackson for her expertise on dealing with post-traumatic stress disorder in children. You're a good friend and I appreciate the great work you perform.

Please forgive any inaccuracies in this story. They are mine alone.

Chapter One

Jillian Russell stared at the meter on the gas pump in stunned disbelief. Holding the nozzle, she listened as the liquid gold rushed into her car's fuel tank. Having just arrived in town, her empty gas tank sucked it in. She figured she should fill up before going home. After Mom's frantic phone call late last night, there was no telling when she might get another chance.

Home. A white-frame house with blue trim in Bartlett, Idaho. The small logging town where Jill had been raised. So small, it didn't even warrant a single traffic light. Population eight hundred and thirty-nine.

Almost everyone here earned their livelihood off of the lush ponderosa pine that blanketed the broad-shouldered mountains surrounding the town. Jill's family included.

"Hi, Jill!"

Lifting her gaze, she looked past the blue pickup truck parked behind her car. Harvey Garson stood outside his grocery store across the deserted street, watering a clay pot filled with purple pansies. The bright flowers did little to hide the peeling paint of his shabby two-story building. Several empty offices lined Main Street, their vacant windows filled with dust and cobwebs. The poor economy hadn't been easy on this community. The bank and county courthouse down the road were new, complete with tan stucco and wide garden boxes planted with yellow tulips. The only modern buildings in town.

Jill waved and forced herself to sound cheerful. "Hello, there."

"You in town long?" Harvey yelled as water cascaded from the spout of his watering can.

She hoped not. But that depended on Mom and Alan, her younger brother by two years. "Just a few days, I think."

"Hopefully we'll see you at church on Sunday." With another wave, Harvey set the watering can beside the flowerpot and slipped back inside his dingy store.

Jill released a sigh of relief, glad the conversation had ended. She hoped she wasn't in town long enough to attend church. She was not staying in this one-dog town any longer than necessary. The dreaded third degree she received from old friends every time she came home was extra incentive not to stick around. You couldn't expect much less in a place this size. Everyone knew everyone else and considered them family. They meant well, but she had no desire to share her life with them. Or explain about her adulterous husband and recent divorce. The pain still felt too raw.

Just then, Larry Newton, a boy she'd graduated from high school with, drove by and honked his horn. At the age of twenty-eight, he wasn't a boy anymore. Not with a wife and two kids.

Forcing a smile to her lips, Jill lifted her hand. She couldn't help feeling that true love and a family of her own had passed her by. After five years of marriage, she'd discovered her ex-husband had cheated on her. Not once, but many times. And then the harshest blow yet.

He'd said he never really loved her at all.

What a fool she'd been. So trusting. So naive. But no more. She was an educated professional woman with a special education career she loved. She didn't need a man. She didn't need anyone. Or at least, she kept telling herself that.

The cumbersome nozzle clicked off and Jill lifted it back into the holding bracket. With a few quick twists of her wrist, she put the cap back on her gas tank. She was determined not to let the cruelty of the past destroy her future. Determined to enjoy her summer break. Maybe being home was the distraction she needed. She wanted consistency in her life. Boring could be good sometimes. And nothing much ever changed in Bartlett.

Nothing except her.

Stepping past the melee of pumps and a tall garbage can, she headed toward the small convenience store to pay her bill.

"Evie! Wait!"

A man's frantic yell drew Jill's attention toward the store. Ignoring the man's plea, a blond-haired girl who looked about six dashed from the store and into the driveway.

Out of her peripheral vision, Jill caught the streak of another car racing toward the child. Without thinking, she lunged into the driveway, scooped the girl into her arms and darted out of harm's way just in time. The driver slammed on his brakes, his car squealing in protest. Jill stood sandwiched between two gas pumps, clutching little Evie to her chest. The driver, a teenage boy with sandy brown hair and freckles, glared his disapproval, then sped on past.

Jill stood there, breathing hard. The full impact of what had almost happened swept over her like a cold, drenching rain. Her heart pounded against her ribs. She tried to swallow, but a dry lump of cotton seemed to have lodged at the base of her throat. Her arms tightened around the little girl as she took a deep, settling breath. Trying to gather her thoughts. Trying to absorb that they were safe.

No harm done.

"Are you okay?" Jill asked against the child's soft hair.

Evie didn't speak. She fisted her hands around Jill's neck like a vise and gulped air into her lungs, hyperventilating with fear. Something had really set her off.

Jill rubbed Evie's back. "Shh, it's okay. You're safe now."

The girl didn't draw back to look at Jill. Didn't let go. Didn't move.

Jill tried to set Evie on her feet, but she gave a pitiful whimper and held on tighter. She wrapped herself around Jill the way a baby gorilla hugs onto its mother. The girl's thin body trembled, her breath whooshing in and out of her lungs like a panicked ventilator. When Evie tucked her face against the curve of her neck, Jill's heart gave a powerful squeeze.

"Evie! Are you okay?" The man reached them, his startling blue eyes filled with panic.

Taking a deep inhale, he reached for the girl. Evie tightened her arms around Jill's neck in a stranglehold. She wasn't ready to budge.

Jill tried to pretend she didn't see the guarded hurt in the man's eyes, followed by an expression of vulnerability. If this was his daughter, Evie's rejection must sting him pretty hard.

"She's not letting go," Jill told him, a self-conscious laugh slipping from her throat.

Taken off balance by the girl's weight, Jill tottered backward. She bumped against a bucket sitting beside the gas pump. Grimy water sloshed over the sides. A squeegee for washing windows bobbed around in the brackish liquid.

"I'm sorry about this." The man clasped Jill's arm to steady her before whisking the bucket out of her way.

With Evie facing her and literally sitting in her lap, Jill slid down to the ground. She perched on the ledge of cement beside the two nearest gas pumps and tucked her sandaled feet back toward the island in case another car zipped past. The last thing she needed right now was a broken foot.

"Thank you for rescuing Evie." The man scooped up Jill's purse from out of the driveway and set it beside her. Then, he raked his fingers through his thick, dark hair, making it stand on end.

The light stubble on his blunt chin showed that he hadn't shaved that morning. Not surprising, if he was a logger. But Jill knew almost everyone in town. This guy was new and she couldn't help wondering who he was.

"You're welcome." Jill sat there, stunned. Not knowing what to think about this odd situation she'd been thrust into. Thankfully, as a special-education teacher, her work with autistic and developmentally disabled children in the public school system had taught her patience. Now that Evie was out of danger, Jill knew what to do.

"Why don't we just sit here and catch our breath for a few moments?" she suggested.

The man stepped past the island and leaned one broad shoulder against a gas pump. He towered over her in awkward silence, shifting restlessly, as though he didn't know what to do. Finally, he sat beside her and leaned his elbows on his knees. He stared at her sandals and pink-painted toes for several moments. His handsome mouth quirked into a nervous laugh.

"She hates gas stations," he said. "I shouldn't have taken her inside the store with me, but I couldn't leave her out in the truck all alone."

Jill had no idea why a gas station would cause such an adverse reaction in a young child. For all she knew, Evie was throwing a temper tantrum after her father told her she couldn't buy a piece of candy. But Jill sensed it wasn't quite that simple.

She turned her face toward the quivering child, speaking gently. "I hate gas stations, too. They're usually smelly, dirty places."

The man shook his head, his beautiful blue eyes creased with sorrow. He opened and closed his mouth, as if he wanted to say something, but couldn't quite get the words out. Finally, he spoke quickly. "Actually, her mother was killed inside a gas station convenience store. That's why Evie doesn't like them."

Jill's brain stumbled to a halt and she blinked her eyes. "Oh. I'm sorry to hear that."

A surge of sympathy pinched her heart. Knowing this personal bit of information made her feel even more protective of Evie. At the same time, a barrage of questions pummeled Jill's mind. The special-education teacher in her rose to the forefront. She'd like to know more about Evie's problem but didn't think it was her place to ask.

"I'm Brent Knowles. Evie's father." The man thrust out one of his large, calloused hands.

Jill lifted her right hand off Evie's back long enough for Brent to shake it. "My name's Jill. Glad to meet you."

"I'm sorry to impose on you like this, Jill." Brent reached to take Evie again, his powerful fingers engulfing the girl's thin arms.

In response, Evie's hold constricted around Jill's neck and she shook her head. She didn't want to leave yet.

"Let her stay with me for a few more minutes. She's still trembling," Jill said.

Brent let go and didn't argue the point. Jill fought off a wave of discomfort. After all, these people were complete strangers to her. They were probably passing through town and had stopped to fill up their gas tank. But Evie's behavior wasn't normal for a child of her age. No, not at all.

"How old are you, Evie?" Jill spoke against the girl's warm cheek, trying to take her mind off whatever had upset her.

No response.

Jill tried again. "What grade are you in?"

Still nothing.

"She doesn't speak. Not since her mother

was killed last year during an armed robbery," Brent whispered reluctantly.

Oh, dear. It seemed Evie's problem was more serious than Jill had first thought. And Jill couldn't suppress a desire to help. This was a unique situation she found herself in. Without hearing any more details, she would have diagnosed Evie with post-traumatic stress disorder. Of course, Jill wasn't a medical professional, but she *was* trained in how to help kids cope with difficult problems in their lives. Even if that didn't translate to her personal life. With her skill set, she should at least be able to manage her own woes. But she hadn't been able to. At least, not yet.

"Did you see what happened to your mom?" Jill whispered to Evie.

In response, the child buried her face deeper against Jill's shoulder. That was answer enough. Jill had no doubt Evie was suffering from PTSD, brought on by witnessing her mother's violent death. Something no child should ever see. No doubt the trauma had caused Evie's selective mutism, too. The girl had been literally scared silent.

It was bad enough for a kid to lose her mom, but to actually witness her mother's death made it even worse.

"Don't worry. You're safe now. We can sit here for as long as you like," Jill told the girl.

Evie's hold on Jill's neck relaxed just a bit.

"You seem good with kids," Brent said.

She nodded. "I have a master's degree in special education and teach for the Boise School District."

His mouth went slack. "Evie isn't a special-ed kid. She's very intelligent. She just saw something really bad."

He sounded defensive and Jill figured he'd dealt with people thinking Evie was mentally challenged because she wouldn't speak. Because of his protectiveness toward his daughter, Jill liked him immediately.

"I'm sure she's very smart. She's just experienced a terrible trauma, which is why she's chosen to be silent." Jill hugged the girl closer, wishing she could somehow shield Evie from being hurt again.

Life could be so unkind.

"Most people don't understand. They think Evie should just get over it and start talking again," Brent said.

Jill shrugged. "Well, I understand. Many disabled people are very bright. They simply have a unique issue they have to work through. And sometimes that takes a very long time. But most people are impatient creatures. They want answers now and aren't always willing to work for it."

His blue eyes crinkled at the corners as he looked at her with awe. "You really do understand, don't you?"

Jill smiled, thinking it all sounded so easy when she talked about it like this. But real life was actually a very messy affair. Not so easy when you had to wade through the muck and figure things out on your own. If God hadn't abandoned her after the divorce, she might not feel so alone now. But He had and she did.

"Are you from around here?" he asked.

"Yes, I grew up here and still consider it home. My family lives in town. Since the school year ended yesterday in Boise, and I'm off for the summer, I decided to come back for a visit."

"Ah."

For another five minutes, she sat there with Evie's very tall, muscular father hovering over her. She took a moment to study him without appearing to do so. Long legs sheathed in faded blue jeans and worn cowboy boots. He had startling blue eyes and saber-sharp cheekbones. Highly attractive. In his eyes, she saw his concern and anxiety—and all the love he had for his daughter. He was the kind of guy that made her think maybe love hadn't passed her by after all. That maybe she should reconsider dating and give love one more chance.

No! She mentally shook her head, telling herself she wasn't interested. Not in any man. Not ever again. Her heart couldn't take it.

"Evie, can you be really brave and let go of me now?" Jill finally asked the girl.

Evie drew back and gazed at her. She had a cute button nose and blue, translucent eyes identical to her father's.

"Do you feel better?" Jill asked her.

Evie nodded, but she didn't speak. She simply looked deep into Jill's eyes, as though peering into her soul. Jill felt as though this innocent child were assessing each and every one of her flaws and determining if she was worthy of her trust.

"Do you think you can go with your father now?" Jill said.

Another nod. The girl slid off Jill's lap and reached for her daddy's hand. Brent pulled Evie into his arms, kissing her face several times, brushing the long, blond hair back from her cheeks as he whispered a contrite apology. And once again, his actions toward his daughter made Jill like this man on the spot.

"I'm so sorry, sweetheart. I shouldn't have made you go inside the store with me," he whispered.

Jill watched the pair closely, feeling out of place as she witnessed this poignant moment between father and daughter. Evie clung to her dad and nodded her forgiveness. The two obviously had a close relationship.

Jill stood, stretching her numb legs and brushing a streak of dirt off her blue jeans.

"Sorry to trouble you, Jill. Thanks again." Brent held out his hand.

Jill shook it, the warmth of his fingers sending an electric pulse up her arm. She quickly let go, her stomach churning. "Anytime."

She stood back as he led Evie to his truck and helped the little girl climb inside.

Picking up her purse, Jill went into the store. As she paid her gas bill and explained to the gawking sales clerk what had happened, she couldn't help wondering about Evie and her worried father. If they were passing through town, Jill would never see them again. If they lived in Bartlett, they were bound to meet up somewhere. Maybe at the grocery store, or the one-room post office. Of course, Jill wasn't planning to stay long. A few days. A couple of months, max. It depended on how bad the problems were at her family's business. She'd soothe her mother's frayed nerves, try to help her younger brother at the sawmill and repair the damage if she could, then return to her lonely apartment in Boise. Evie and Brent Knowles were simply strangers that had crashed into Jill's life and were now gone.

And that was that.

Brent opened the truck door and helped Evie climb into her seat. After buckling her in, he paused long enough to gaze into her mournful eyes. He cupped her rosy cheek with the palm of his hand and kissed the tip of her nose.

"You okay now, honey?" he asked.

She didn't return his smile, just gazed back at him with a somber expression. Sometimes he wished she'd yell and scream. That was something he could understand. Something he thought he knew how to handle. But this quiet compliance, he couldn't comprehend. It made him wonder what was going on in his little girl's mind. Her silent solitude must be such an empty, lonely place. If only she'd let him in. If only she would trust him. He felt so clumsy and inept at helping her forget the trauma of her mother's death.

So powerless.

His prayers remained unanswered. No matter what he did, he couldn't break through the hushed walls Evie had erected around herself. Even after taking her to a barrage of doctors and specialists, Brent still didn't know how to help his own little girl.

"You feeling better?" he asked again.

She gave a tentative nod, her gaze sliding toward the convenience store where Jill was paying her bill.

"You like her, don't you?" he asked.

Evie nodded again.

"Me, too. She's a nice lady."

And she'd been there for his daughter. A complete stranger. But a pretty stranger. She was a petite woman with long, sandy-blond hair and intelligent amber-colored eyes. And when she'd flashed her dazzling smile, it had made his throat constrict. Even now, he could hardly take his eyes off her and kept glancing over to view her through the store windows. She'd been so patient and kind, not rushing Evie the way her teachers and counselors sometimes tried to do. And not one of them had gotten through to Evie. No one had.

Until today.

Closing the door, Brent walked around to the driver's seat and climbed inside. Jill's car was parked in front of his vehicle, so he took his time. Rather than backing out, he'd wait for her to pull forward.

Evie never took her hawkish gaze off him, vigilant to ensure he didn't leave her. As he started the engine, he switched the heater on low. The spring weather had put a distinct chill in the air.

He looked at the convenience store. Jill walked toward her car, reaching to take her keys out of her purse. She glanced his way, her warm eyes meeting his. All at once, her cheeks flooded with color and she ducked her head, obviously embarrassed by what had transpired between them. She opened her car door, seeming eager to escape.

Brent couldn't blame her. She must be feeling a bit jittery after what had happened. An unfamiliar man and his daughter clinging to her like they were all close friends. And a part of him wished he didn't have to leave it like this. Not without clarifying things first. Not without knowing more about Jill. He was quickly forgetting that she was a stranger he'd met twenty minutes earlier. For some crazy reason, he felt as though he'd known her all his life.

In her rush, Jill dropped her purse, the contents spilling across the dirty pavement. Her mouth fell open in exasperation and she crouched down to gather up her stuff. A hairbrush, nail file and a wallet with a pink flower decorating the front. Feminine things that reminded Brent she was an attractive woman and he was now a lonely, single father.

He almost got out to help, but thought better of it. He needed to focus on Evie and her needs, not on a pretty special-ed teacher from Boise. With his daughter and busy profession, he had his hands full already. Until Evie was speaking again, he couldn't contemplate anything but her.

Jill glanced up at him and gave an apologetic shrug for the delay. He smiled his encouragement, his mind churning with memories.

He thought about his wife, Lina, and the night she'd died. He'd been working out of town at the time. Fighting wildfire in the mountains of Colorado.

His stomach clenched at the thought. Lina hadn't been feeling well. She'd never asked, but he knew she wanted him to stay home with her. He'd left anyway. The overtime and hazard pay were too much to resist. He didn't make a large salary and the extra money would allow them to pay off some bills.

How Brent wished he'd remained home with his family. An inferno of regret scorched his gut every time he thought that maybe, if he hadn't gone on the wildfire, Lina would still be alive. She'd be whole and unhurt. Evie would be okay. The burden of guilt weighed heavy on his heart. And with Evie refusing to speak, he couldn't seem to shake it off.

Giving another, yet more exasperated shrug, Jill stood and opened her car door before slinging her purse onto the passenger seat. He chuckled, wishing he dared roll down his window and tease her about all the heavy bags women seemed to carry around everywhere they went. But then, he froze, realizing this was the first time since Lina's death that he'd felt like flirting with a woman.

His mind stumbled to a halt. Confused and empty. Wondering what was wrong with him. Wondering what it was about Jill that appealed to him so strongly. Perhaps it was just her kindness toward Evie. And yet, he knew it was something more. Something he couldn't explain. Like an invisible magnet that drew him to her in spite of his vow never to love again.

As Jill climbed inside her car, she flashed that stunning smile of hers and waved at Evie. Brent looked back at his daughter and witnessed the greatest marvel of all. Something Brent never expected and hadn't seen in a very long time.

Evie smiled and waved back.

Chapter Two

"No, I don't have an appointment with the forest ranger, but I still need to see him. Right now." Jill stood inside the reception room of the redbrick Forest Service office, gripping the strap of her blue leather purse with whitened knuckles.

Martha Hartnett, the receptionist, stared at her with wide eyes. Jill met the older woman's gaze without flinching. Feeling determined and forceful. Unwilling to leave this office until she got the answers she needed.

"I'll ask if he can see you," Martha murmured as she walked around the high counter, and headed down the long hallway toward the back offices.

Jill watched her go, feeling shameful for her pushy behavior. Martha's husband worked at the sawmill and Jill hated upsetting the woman. This situation wasn't Martha's fault. But Jill was exhausted. She'd spent a sleepless night, sitting up with her anguished mother, trying to sort through everything her brother had told her. Accusations against Alan that didn't make sense.

At least, not to her.

Jill didn't know what to believe right now. Alan had always been a good kid. Hardworking and generous. And he'd proven it when Dad had died eight months earlier. While Jill lived in Boise with a career she loved and the aftershocks of a broken heart, Alan had stepped in to take on full management of Russell Sawmill without a single complaint. Timber harvest had been here in Bartlett since the early 1900s, when Teddy Roosevelt and his army of forest rangers had demanded the preservation of large tracts of land for future generations. Jill's great-great-grandfather had built Russell Sawmill and never left town. But Jill had—as fast as she could go. The moment she'd graduated from high school. After all, what kind of future would she have had here? None. Unless she'd wanted to work at the sawmill the rest of her life. Which she hadn't—and still didn't.

It was a two-and-a-half hour drive from Bartlett to the nearest doctor, dentist and decent shopping in the city of Boise. She pacified her guilt for not coming home often by telling herself it was too far to drive frequently. And since leaving Bartlett, she'd returned only for Christmas holidays, short summer vacations, her father's funeral and to help occasionally at the mill.

Until now.

Alan was only twenty-six. Though she was proud that he'd taken it on, he was too young for so much responsibility. The whole family knew he wasn't much of a businessman when it came to balancing the books, but Alan knew logging and how to run the timber yard. If not for her brother taking over the mill operations, they might have had to sell it off. Or worse yet, shut their doors. With dozens of employees depending upon the sawmill for their livelihood, they just couldn't close up shop. But now, Alan had been accused of something dreadful.

Timber theft.

A charge that could destroy their family's reputation and put their entire sawmill out of operation. Jill couldn't let that happen. Alan claimed he was innocent. And to find out the truth, Jill had to speak with the forest ranger. She had to know why he believed Alan had stolen hundreds of thousands of dollars' worth of ponderosa pine.

"Jill?"

Jerking around, she came face-to-face with Brent Knowles. He stood inside the doorway, his sun-bronzed features creased with confusion. In a quick glance, her gaze swept over his handsome face, then down past his drab olive-colored shirt and spruce-green pants. Her gaze focused on the bronze shield pinned to the left front pocket of his shirt. In a rush, her stomach cramped with uncertainty and a tight breath whispered past her lips.

Forest ranger.

Inwardly, Jill groaned. Recognition flashed through her brain like lightning across the mountains. Brent was the ranger. Evie's daddy. The man that had made Jill think about dating and giving love a second chance. The same man that had accused Jill's brother of stealing timber from the national forest.

Jill blinked, trying to absorb the truth with her dazed brain. Surely Brent couldn't be the same person who had soothed Evie so tenderly the day before.

Or could he?

For several moments, she couldn't contain her surprise. Her mouth dropped open and her eyes narrowed. "Y-you're the forest ranger?"

Her voice sounded small and uncertain. She'd been gone from home long enough that they must have changed forest rangers on her.

The last ranger she'd worked with at her family's sawmill had been short and portly, with a large belly that jiggled over his belt buckle when he walked. Overbellie, they'd called him. Not this tall, gorgeous man with a friendly smile that turned her brain to mush. Right now, she felt as though the air had been sucked out of the room.

"Yes, I'm the ranger." Brent nodded, tilting his head to one side as he looked at her quizzically. No doubt, he was wondering what she was doing here. And why she'd so rudely demanded to see him.

"Oh." Her voice sounded like a deflating balloon.

"You look upset. Why don't you come back to my office so we can talk?" He stepped back, waiting for her to precede him down the hall.

For the count of three, Jill hesitated. Every harsh word she'd planned to say to this man who'd thrown suspicion on her brother froze on the tip of her tongue. As she took a step, she remembered Evie and that the little girl had lost her mother in a violent tragedy.

That Brent had also lost his wife.

Jill didn't speak as she headed down the hall like a stealth bomber on a collision course. She knew the way. Over the years, she'd been here often enough. First, with her father, when he'd taught her and Alan how to run the sawmill. But she'd never liked this place, because the forest ranger had the authority to tell her family when and where they could harvest timber for their mill. He was the enemy. At least, that's what had been ingrained in Jill since birth. Rangers and loggers were not friends. Not ever. It was that simple.

Then, after Dad had died, she'd helped with the transition at the mill, until Alan took it over. But she'd never had plans to return. She should be with her husband right now. Happy and in love. Planning a family of her own. Instead, she felt disillusioned and cynical. At first, she'd blamed her failed marriage on herself. She'd been so busy with her education and then work. When she'd learned David had been cheating on her for years, she couldn't help wondering why her husband hadn't wanted her. If David had loved her, she would have tried to make it work. But he didn't, and they'd divorced three months before her father died.

The sound of a phone ringing and the click of someone typing in one of the back offices filled the void. Jill took that moment to gather her thoughts, but found herself wishing again that she hadn't come here. Maybe it would have been better to disregard the rumors of theft that were flaming around town and let it all die down. But Jill feared ignoring them might only allow the situation to escalate. She must deal with it now, before it became worse. If nothing else, she needed to ease her mother's frantic mind.

"Have a seat." Brent touched her arm as he indicated one of the cushioned chairs sitting in front of a wide mahogany desk in his modest office.

Jill sat and rubbed the spot where he'd grazed her, the warmth of his fingers still lingering. She glanced at a row of metal filing cabinets, a scenic picture of a mule deer, and piles of manila folders. Her gaze screeched to a halt on a picture of a younger Evie sitting on the desk. The girl was laughing, cuddled against a smiling woman with the same chin and golden hair. No doubt it was Evie's mother, Brent's deceased wife.

Jill couldn't believe the difference in Evie. She looked so happy and carefree in the picture. Like a normal, exuberant little girl. Not at all the frightened, haunted child Jill had met at the gas station yesterday afternoon.

"So, what can I do for you?" Brent slid the picture around as he perched on one corner of the desk. Jill sensed it was a protective gesture. A subtle way of keeping his life private. A barrier to keep Jill out.

Okay, she could take the hint. In fact, she preferred it that way, too.

He braced one long leg against the floor, his other leg bent at the knee and swinging free. Completely masculine and attractive. And she was trying very hard not to stare.

Jill cleared her throat. "I've come to ask about your accusations against my brother."

He cocked his head to one side. "Your brother?"

"Yes, Alan Russell."

Dawning flooded his face. "So you're Al's sister?"

"Yes." Something hardened inside of her. Yesterday, she'd wanted to help Brent Knowles and his little girl. But right now, she was interested in protecting her own family. She squelched her sentimental feelings, determined to keep her loyalties straight. Family came first.

"I'm afraid I don't understand," he said.

"You've made accusations against him."

He stared at her in stony silence. Then, he stood and walked around to his chair, placing the obstacle of his desk between them. He sat down and crossed his infinitely long legs, seeming to choose his words carefully. "That isn't true, Jill. No accusations have been made against your brother, or anyone else for that matter. At least, not by the Forest Service."

"But there's been gossip around town that you believe Alan is stealing timber. A lot of gossip."

A serene smile of tolerance played at the corners of his full mouth. She sensed that he was trying to be polite but still had to do his job.

"I'm afraid we don't build cases of theft off of town gossip," he said. "And even if we did, I wouldn't be able to discuss the case with you."

His words placed another blockade between them. It felt odd after yesterday, when he'd been so forthcoming about Evie's problem. She wanted to like this man but realized that might be impossible now.

"Since I own a half interest in the sawmill, I have a right to know what's going on," she said.

He took a deep inhale, the expanse of his chest widening even further, if that were possible. "I can understand your frustration. But at this point, all we know is that a lot of timber has been harvested illegally from Cove Mountain. We don't know for sure who the guilty party might be. No charges have been made against anyone. Yet."

Yet. That single word echoed through the room like a shout and the silence thickened.

She quirked one brow. "Then, you haven't told any of your employees that you believe Alan is the thief? And that you plan to prosecute him to the fullest extent of the law?"

That's what Mom had claimed last night as Jill had tried to soothe her tears. But then again, Mom frequently blew situations like this out of proportion. Hence, Jill had decided to learn the truth.

He hesitated. "The discussions that take place between me and my employees are confidential. I don't know where you've gotten your information, but it's not correct. Right now, I don't know who the guilty party is."

Jill's shoulders stiffened. She'd seen this scenario before during her childhood. The assumption would be that the owner of the sawmill was in on the theft. And in such a small town as Bartlett, gossip spread like wildfire. Hearing that her brother was a thief didn't sit well with Jill. No, not at all.

"What do you intend to do about the situation?" she asked.

"I'm not at liberty to discuss it with you right now. But I can tell you that I've called in the LEI to perform an investigation."

Oh no! The LEI was the Forest Service's

Law Enforcement and Investigation unit. Jill bit the inside of her cheek to hide her panic. She knew the drill. A special agent would come to Bartlett and investigate the theft. No doubt her family's sawmill would bear the brunt of the inquiry. And if they didn't cooperate, Alan would look even more guilty.

"Then, you don't currently have plans to charge my brother with a crime?" she asked.

He sat back, his chair squeaking. "No, not at this time."

"I can understand why you've called for an investigation, but do you have any reason to believe Alan is responsible?"

"Not yet. Large tracts of ponderosa pine have been harvested in the mountains bordering the cutblock where your mill was contracted to cut trees. The thieves decimated the area, leaving nothing for the future. That's all I can tell you at this time."

Her heart plummeted. All it took was for Martha, or one of Brent's other employees, to talk about the theft at the dinner table with their family, and news soon spread. It wouldn't even do Jill any good to ask who the gossip might have come from. It could be anyone. It didn't matter, now. Chances were she'd known the culprit all her life and they were friends. And threatening Brent with a slander lawsuit wasn't Jill's style. She didn't like contention. Besides, she couldn't prove it and doubted it would go anywhere. But she still needed to do some damage control.

She held his gaze for several pounding moments. He lifted his chin in challenge.

"So, because my family's sawmill was contracted to cut timber near the area where the trees were stolen, you think my brother is guilty of the theft. You don't know for certain?"

He released a soft sigh. "Again, I don't think anything right now. No accusations have…"

"I know, I know. No accusations have been made against anyone yet." She cut him off with a wave of her hand.

His expression softened with empathy. "I'm sorry, Jill. I can't say anything more. But rest assured I'll contact you about it as soon as I can."

His eyes darkened to a steely blue and she heard the soft edge of professionalism in his voice. He didn't like this situation any more than she did. But that wouldn't stop him from pursuing an investigation. Which might incriminate Alan and destroy the mill. Since Brent hadn't made any formal accusations against Alan, she couldn't really ask what evidence he might already have on her brother. Not if she expected a genuine answer.

For the first time, Jill felt an edge of uncertainty. Late last night, Alan had told her and Mom that he was innocent. But what if he'd lied to them? He'd always been so honest. So kind and generous. But everyone had their limits. In this rotten economy, the construction industry had been hit hard. Meeting their payroll and other bills had become difficult. Could Alan have become desperate enough to start pilfering timber? Jill knew he'd do almost anything to keep Mom safe. But did that include theft and lying to cover it up?

She hauled in a deep breath, her mind a jumble of unease. No, Alan wouldn't do such a thing. Would he?

She didn't like the pang of suspicion that nibbled at her mind. Maybe it was time she went down to the sawmill office and took a look at the books herself. It'd been months since she'd worked there, and she had to know what was going on. If for no other reason than to help reassure her agitated mother that her only son wasn't going to lose their family business and end up in prison.

Brent gazed at Jill with regret. A blaze of compassion sliced through his heart, but he ignored the urge to blurt out the truth. He couldn't compromise this case. There was too much to lose. Including his livelihood. He liked Jill Russell. A lot. But he also had a job to do. And that must come first. "I'm sorry about this situation, Jill. I truly am. But the gossip didn't come from me."

"So, what are we supposed to do now?" she asked.

He caught the twinge of hurt in her voice and hated it. For some reason, he felt protective of this woman and longed to shield her from this problem. "Anything you like."

"You really can't tell me something more?"

"Not right now. As soon as I can, I promise to give you a call." Brent met her gaze, trying to concentrate. The naked fear in her eyes haunted him, along with the sweet fragrance of her hair. He took a deep inhale, drawn to this woman in spite of the warning sirens going off inside his head. After her kindness to him and Evie yesterday afternoon, he wasn't being much help. Of course Jill was worried about her brother and the sawmill. It was only natural. And Brent blamed himself.

"How long will the investigation take?" she asked.

"I don't know."

It would be unprofessional for him to tell her

that timber theft was difficult to prove and the conviction rate was low. That was good for the thieves and bad for the victims of the crime, which in this case were the taxpayers.

She stood, bracing one hand against the armrest of her chair. She looked shaky and he reached out to clasp her arm and steady her. She flinched and he let go, wishing he could offer her more reassurance. That he could say something to put her at ease. But he couldn't. Not yet, anyway.

He accompanied her to the door. "Thanks for stopping by."

"Thanks for seeing me," she said.

"Anytime. My door is always open to you." And he meant it. He owed her that much.

She stepped out. He planned to follow her to the outer reception area, but she held up a hand. "I know the way. I'll see myself out."

As she walked down the hallway, he stared after her, thinking she had the longest legs he'd ever seen on a woman. Wishing he could call her back. Yearning to tell her all the facts. But his job prohibited it. Too much was riding on this case and he couldn't jeopardize it by confiding in her.

Instead, Brent returned to his desk. Reaching for his keyboard, he rapped out a quick email to his staff members. First thing in the morning, he'd hold a quick meeting with all his employees to discuss the importance of confidentiality. No doubt one of his people had seen the investigation request he'd filed with the LEI, or overheard a conversation he'd had with his timber assistant about the stolen trees. Not once had Brent mentioned the Russell Sawmill in connection with the theft, but conjecture was bound to occur. Someone had assumed Alan Russell was to blame for the theft, and word had soon spread.

That wasn't what was troubling Brent right now. He'd done his best to alleviate Jill's concerns. But the truth was, Alan had already come forward to seek Brent's help. Eight weeks earlier, the man had walked into Brent's office and claimed he was being blackmailed by Frank Casewell, his mill manager. According to Alan, Frank was stealing the timber late at night and processing it at the sawmill to sell on the black market. If Alan turned Frank in, Frank had threatened to burn the sawmill to the ground. Which was something Frank had supposedly admitted to doing to another sawmill three years earlier in Missoula, Montana. No doubt Frank had threatened Alan in order to frighten him into keeping his mouth shut. But it hadn't worked. Alan had fretted over the problem for two months, but he'd finally come forward, anxious to help convict Frank and protect his family's business.

Now they needed proof. Evidence that would allow them to arrest Frank. If they could catch him and his accomplices in the act of stealing timber, they'd get a conviction. Otherwise, it was Alan's word against Frank's word.

Since he'd been working for the Forest Service in Montana at the time, Brent knew about the sawmill that had been burned three years earlier. A good friend of his had died in that fire and he was eager to obtain any evidence that would convict the culprit of murder. The fact that Alan had brought the matter to the authorities spoke highly of his integrity. But he'd still waited two months. Brent didn't trust Alan either. Not completely. Until he had more evidence one way or the other, Brent planned to proceed with caution. He didn't want the situation to get out of hand, but neither would he let down his guard until he had evidence to convict Frank.

Brent had already contacted the US Attorney's office on Alan's behalf. They were now working together to set up a sting operation to catch the guilty party. Unfortunately, Brent couldn't tell Jill all of that. And neither could Alan. If he talked with anyone about the case, including his family, the deal with the

US Attorney's office was void. They couldn't take the risk of letting others in on the plan as it might jeopardize them snagging Frank and his band of thieves. It was that simple and that serious. So they must wait on the LEI's investigation.

And it was unfortunate for him that he'd lost Jill's trust by denying her any more information. He'd wanted to put her at ease and keep her as a friend. Brent had been thinking of tracking her down and asking if she might help him with Evie. All he knew was that Jill was trained in special education and Evie had responded to her like no one else.

Under the circumstances, that plan seemed futile now. No doubt Jill wouldn't take kindly to him asking her to work with his little girl. After all, he was the evil forest ranger. For most loggers, being the ranger was a similitude for being the Big Bad Wolf.

The enemy. Someone they could never trust.

Heaving a disgruntled sigh, Brent stood and walked down the dingy hallway to the watercooler. The modest offices of this forest district weren't fancy, but it was Brent's first ranger assignment. There were fewer than four hundred rangers nationwide, so it was an honor to get this job. Previously, he'd been a fire specialist at another national forest in Montana.

He loved it here in Idaho and wanted so much to succeed. And he didn't want to alienate the pretty sawmill owner in the process.

The spout gurgled as he filled a plastic cup with clear liquid and downed it in three quick gulps. The cup made a low popping sound as he crumpled it in his hand and tossed it into the garbage can. Two points.

He didn't dare ask for Jill's assistance, but he had to help Evie somehow. He couldn't lose her to the silent world she'd built around herself. She had a right to lead a normal, happy life like other kids her age. To grow up feeling secure. He'd tried everything he could think of and it hadn't been enough. But he'd never quit on his child. Never give up hope.

Sauntering back to his office, he closed his door, wanting no interruptions while he considered what he should do. Sitting in his high-backed faux-leather chair, he ignored the creaking hinges as he leaned back and crossed his legs. He picked up a file of pictures his timber assistant had taken of the area where hundreds of ponderosa pine had been cut illegally.

The thieves had to be removing the timber at night, when no one would see their crime. Big trucks like that would be noticed coming down off the mountain during the daytime. But at night, the darkness would help conceal the theft. The work would require accomplices. Several people working together to cut, load and drive the stolen logs down to the mill for processing. Alan claimed he didn't know who Frank's conspirators were. That he hadn't participated in the actual theft and he was never at the sawmill when Frank was processing the stolen timber.

For Jill and her mother's sake, Brent hoped that was true.

Closing the file, he thought about the LEI investigator coming into town next week. Jill wouldn't like it, but Brent had to consider the possibility that Alan Russell had been in on the crime from the beginning, but had gotten cold feet and reported the theft. Brent had seen this happen before. It was the most logical explanation. Frank Casewell would have too much trouble processing raw timber without working with someone on the inside. He needed the use of a mill. And who was more likely to have access and motive than one of the owners of Russell Sawmill?

Brent's gaze swerved to the picture of Evie and her mom. He'd considered asking Jill out. On a real date. The first since before he'd married his wife. But that was no longer a possibility. Not after his jarring conversation with her this morning. Not as long as he posed any kind of threat to her brother.

Earlier that day, Brent had felt an inkling of hope for Evie. The first in over a year. Like God had finally answered his prayers and sent him someone to help his child. But now, that hope was dashed and all Brent felt was frustrated despair.

Chapter Three

"Ida, can you get me the rest of the receivables, please?" Jill called to the front-office manager as she closed yet another file of invoices.

Sitting inside the shabby office at Russell Sawmill, Jill glanced up at the rustic accommodations. A main reception room with a front counter built by her father over twenty years earlier partitioned several old, metal flight desks where the clerical staff performed their daily work. Ida and another clerk occupied this domain, with Jill sitting in the far back corner. Alan had moved into Dad's office. Frank Casewell, the new mill manager Alan had hired shortly after Dad's death, inhabited the second office. The building also included a large conference room with a long, scarred table for meetings.

Sunlight fought its way through the coating of grime and sawdust on the windows. Jill made a mental note to clean them tomorrow morning. The threadbare carpet needed to be replaced, too. It was a pity Alan hadn't renovated the office when he'd decided to spend two million dollars buying new technology for the mill.

And that was another problem. Alan had over-extended them in debt.

Ida handed Jill several files of invoices, her brows furrowed with concern. At the age of forty-seven, Ida was a proficient worker who had been at the mill for over fifteen years. She knew the accounts receivable like the back of her hand. The payables, too. And the latest OSHA regulations from the US Department of Labor.

"We're too far in debt, aren't we?" the matronly woman whispered low, for Jill's ears alone. She cast a surreptitious glance over her plump shoulder at Karen, the pretty part-time clerk, who was busy answering phones.

"I'm afraid so." It did no good to pretend. Not with Ida. She was smart and capable and had long ago proven she could keep a confidence.

Jill released a pensive sigh and pasted a

smile on her face. "But we've been through rougher times than this."

At least, Jill thought they had.

"I don't know when," Ida said.

Jill's heart plunged. That wasn't what she wanted to hear right now. Especially from someone she trusted. Having her fears voiced out loud made her entire body quake.

Ida patted Jill's shoulder with reassurance. "Don't worry. We'll get through this."

That helped a teensy bit, but Jill hoped Ida was right. Until he'd died of a heart attack, Dad had always shielded his family from the careworn worries of the mill. Jill didn't want to alarm her mother or the mill employees, for fear more gossip might spread. In this rotten economy, everyone naturally assumed the mill was struggling, but Jill didn't want to confirm their doubts.

Jill rifled through a packet of overdue invoices. New flexible band saws, conveyors, scanners, lasers and even a bar-coding system to track inventory. Great for output, but very expensive. The mill was bringing in just enough to meet both the payroll and their monthly bills. They sure didn't need a timber theft accusation to top everything off.

Two huge logging trucks lumbered past the windows. Jill whipped her head around to look. From her vantage point, she saw Alan pop up from his desk and saunter out to the front reception area.

"It's sure good to have you back, sis." He leaned against the doorjamb and smiled, a jagged thatch of hair falling across his high forehead.

Jill's heart squeezed. No matter how old or tall he got, Alan was still her kid brother and she loved him so much. "It's good to be home."

And she meant it. It felt good to help in some small way.

"A new load just came in. Guess I better get out there to count it." Alan gestured toward the door.

"Don't forget this." Ida handed him his cell phone.

A reminder that he was on call 24/7. Dad had refused to carry a cell, preferring a clunky black radio they called *the brick*. He'd resisted new technology like the plague. But even without a cell phone, he'd always been at the right place at the right time, seeming to know instinctively what everyone needed from him. And Jill missed him now more than ever.

"Thanks." With a quick grin, Alan tucked the phone into his pocket, scooped up his yellow hard hat, and left the office.

Karen's admiring gaze followed after him

like a love-struck schoolgirl and Jill smiled with amusement.

She tried to tell herself everything was going to be fine, but she was worried. The financials didn't look good and an ugly question kept pounding her brain. Had Alan become desperate enough for money that he'd stooped to stealing timber?

Jill had to find out the truth, and fast.

Forty minutes later, she was waiting for her brother when he returned. She gestured toward his office and he headed that way.

"Ida, we don't want to be disturbed for a while," he told the woman.

Ida gave a solemn nod of understanding.

Inside his office, Alan plopped down in his chair and leaned back. Jill closed the door and sat in a chair across from him.

He looked up and released a heavy sigh. "So, what's the verdict?"

"You already know. We're heavily in debt. Over the past eight months, you've spent almost two million dollars on new technology."

He blinked and licked his dry lips. "Yeah, but our output has doubled. The mill needed to be modernized, Jill. The new equipment has increased our production like crazy."

"But it's barely enough to cover our bills."

He grinned. "But we are making it. Things

will get better. You'll see. Just give us some more time."

She didn't have much choice. "I also can't account for five hundred thousand dollars. It's like it just disappeared off the books. Any idea where the money went?"

He shook his head. "I guarantee I didn't pocket it. Although I might have made some purchases and forgotten to turn in the receipts to Ida."

Forgetting to turn in five hundred thousand dollars' worth of receipts was beyond unusual. She didn't know if Alan had been reckless, careless, or if they had a bigger problem she didn't understand.

Yet. She'd get to the bottom of it.

"Check again. The money's got to be there somewhere in the books," he said. "And I project the new equipment we bought will pay for itself within three years."

She tossed a financial report on his desk. "I'm not so sure. Look at the balance sheet. All it would take is a minor catastrophe to slow down our production and ruin us."

Heaven help them if Brent Knowles discovered evidence that linked Alan to the stolen timber. The ranger could shut down their timber harvest. They had an inventory of logs, but their workers would go through them fast.

Without logs to process, they'd be out of business. The final straw to break their backs.

Alan stared blankly at the numbers on the report before pushing the papers aside. Jill knew he didn't get the math. He never had. But he knew trees. Douglas fir, ponderosa pine and larch. He had an inner intuition, understanding the grain and how to saw through a single tree trunk to get the most usable board feet. No one was better at his craft.

"I thought modernizing the mill was the best thing for us to do," he said.

"It is, but not all at once. Not when we exceed our ability to pay for the new technology."

"I'm sorry, Jill. I didn't think it would be this bad. I've made some mistakes, but I'm trying to clean them up." His smile dropped away and he clamped his mouth closed, looking determined and shamed all at once.

She studied him. His uneasy glance. The way he opened his mouth, then closed it again, as if he wanted to say something. The furtive looks at the door, as if he wanted to escape. She sensed he was keeping something from her. Something big. And the odd thing about it was that she'd gotten the same vibes from Brent Knowles.

Taking a shallow breath, she met Alan's eyes and sought the truth there. "Al, this is just between you and me. I won't tell a single soul. Not even Mom. But I have to ask once more, and I want the facts. Did you steal that timber to pay the bills?"

"No!" He flew out of his seat and smacked his palms down on the top of the desk so hard that she flinched. His face looked tight and angry, his eyes glaring with outrage. "I told you last night, Jill. I'm not a thief and never agreed to the theft. I wouldn't do it. Dad wouldn't approve. And I would never do anything to shame our father like that."

The mention of their dad's honor caused tears to burn her eyes. She tilted her head, surprised by Alan's choice of words. Something about his tone spoke volumes. "Do you know who the thief is?"

His gaze slid away and he sat back down. "I told you. I had no part in it. I'd rather sell off the mill honestly than besmirch Dad's reputation by stealing timber. Even if we had to sell, we could do that with integrity. It wouldn't be ideal, but I could live with that."

Hmm. He hadn't answered her question. Not really. But all that mattered right now was that he'd claimed he was innocent and she trusted him.

She held up a hand. "Okay, I believe you. But I had to ask. At some point, we may need to hire a lawyer from Boise. But if you say you're innocent, then I'll stand beside you all the way, Allie."

Allie. The childhood nickname she used for him when they were alone.

She meant what she said. Even if she embarrassed herself in the process, she'd defend him. This was her brother, after all. Her family. If nothing else, she was loyal. She'd been pursuing her own goals for long enough. Now Alan and Mom needed her, and she was determined not to let them down.

Alan's features softened, but his brown eyes showed his anxiety. "Thanks, sis. It's bad enough that Mom suspects me of theft. The past months since Dad died have been pretty rough at home. I don't think I can stand it if you believe I'm guilty, too."

Again, her conscience gave a tight pinch. "Don't worry about Mom. I'll speak to her."

Poor Mom. She was still grieving for Dad. They all were.

"Thanks." He gave a weak smile, looking so much like the young boy she'd grown up with.

"Do you know what's inside there?" She pointed at the black twenty-inch safe sitting in one corner of the room. Before his death, this had been Dad's office. The safe had been here as long as Jill could remember, but she'd only seen inside it once or twice.

Alan shrugged. "Just some old bank records. Dad opened it the day before he died, but I lost the key."

"And you haven't opened it since Dad died?"

He shrugged. "Nope. I didn't think it was important."

"Hmm. We should get a locksmith to open it for us. There might be something of value inside."

"I've been meaning to call someone, but knew it'd cost us a pretty penny to have a locksmith drive into town from Boise," he said.

No doubt he was right, but it couldn't be helped. "I'll call in the next week or so and ask what it might cost."

Standing, she went to the door and laid her hand on the knob. She smiled back at him. "I love you, Allie. Don't let these problems eat you up inside. We'll work something out. We just need to figure out what that might be."

"Yeah, you're right." He bobbed his head in a quick series of nods.

"I'm gonna head out now. I'll see you back at home later tonight for supper," she said.

It was time she drove out to Cove Mountain and took a look at the cutblock herself.

She needed to know just how bad the theft really was.

"Okay. See you soon." He waved, looking momentarily like the sweet, naive boy she'd been raised with.

As she stepped into the outer office, she tugged her purse out of the desk drawer where she'd stowed it earlier that morning. A number of possible solutions to their financial woes rumbled through her mind. Solutions that wouldn't involve laying off any workers.

They could sell off some of the new equipment Alan had recently bought, but they wouldn't get full price now. They might be able to refinance their loan, or take out a second mortgage on Mom's house. That meant talking to Larry Cambridge, the bank manager. And Mom would have to sign the papers, which might freak her out in her present state of mind.

Jill took a deep, settling breath. She hoped it wouldn't come to that. Mom's security was important, too. She wouldn't want to move to Boise to live with Jill.

The mill currently specialized in lumber and plywood. Maybe they could diversify into posts and poles. Definitely not ideal, but it might be enough to keep them in the black.

They'd figure something out. She just hoped they didn't lose the sawmill in the process.

Brent flipped on the heater in his truck. The damp May weather didn't bode well for fire season. The heavy rains they'd been having would turn everything to green. Then, as the cheatgrass dried out in June, he could find himself called out on a wildfire. That would mean leaving Evie overnight with Velma Crawford, her sitter. Not an ideal situation, but it couldn't be helped. At least Evie liked Velma and was willing to stay in her home while Brent went to work every day.

Looking across the seat, he smiled at his sweet little daughter sitting serenely in her booster car seat. He'd wanted to take Evie with him up on Cove Mountain, so he'd left his Forest Service truck parked back at his office. Even though he was still working, some people might create a stink if they saw his child riding around with him in a government truck. They didn't understand the long hours a forest ranger worked, so he tried to spend time with his family while he checked the cutblock where Russell Sawmill was harvesting timber.

"You doing okay, sweetheart?" he asked.

Evie didn't smile, but she nodded and gazed out the window as zillions of vibrant green ponderosa pine flashed past their view. A cloud of dust billowed up behind them on the narrow dirt road as they circled the mountain.

He downshifted as they climbed in elevation. Thick forests of Douglas fir, western hemlock and ponderosa pine pierced the azure sky like elegant dancers. A logger's paradise. You sure couldn't get views like this living in a city.

Evie glanced at him and he knew what she was thinking.

"Pretty, isn't it?" he said.

She nodded, a permanent scowl marring her high forehead as she clutched a stuffed toy rabbit in her lap. The way her wary gaze darted between him and the road told him she was excited but nervous. She never quite let down her guard anymore. Never was fully at ease.

A double-trailer logging truck approached from the opposite direction and Brent pulled over on the thin road to give it extra room to pass. Brent returned the driver's wave as his gaze swept the heavy load of ponderosa pine, which towered over the cab of the truck. A flash of red caught his eye. A ticket stapled to one log on the back of the load. It was habit for Brent to look. To inspect. To make sure the loggers were following the law. He knew his timber assistant was working up here today and must have already checked the load of lumber to determine the number of logs.

Back on the road, he soon approached the landing area of the timber operation, and the sound of heavy engines and chain saws filled the air along with suffocating dust. Evie clapped her hands over her ears and scowled at the deafening noise. Brent chuckled as they passed by the cutblock area. Another fifteen minutes and he pulled over and killed the engine. He didn't like what he saw. From the disapproving scowl on her face, neither did Evie.

Dozens of naked stumps porcupined the mountainside. Gone were the tall, lush trees that used to blanket this hillside, cut and stolen in the night by thieves.

Evie reached across the seat and tugged on his sleeve. He looked her way and she pointed out the window. A lone figure moved through the ruined forest. A woman, wearing blue jeans and a red sweater.

Jill!

Before he could stop her, Evie clicked off her seat belt, threw open the heavy door and hopped out of the truck.

"Evie, wait," he called as she raced toward Jill.

Brent hurried to follow after his daughter. Since the theft, an eerie silence filled this forest with nothingness. No birdsong. No animal life. No treetops rustling as the breeze rippled past. This forest had been destroyed.

Violated by greed.

At the sounds of Evie's running feet and gasping breath, Jill turned and gazed at the child with wide-eyed surprise.

"Evie. What are you doing here?" Jill said.

She lifted her head. Brent was highly aware of the exact moment when she saw him. He felt her gaze like a physical blow. As though an electric current flowed between them, shocking him with its intensity. And he couldn't ignore a sudden rush of joy. For some inane reason, he liked being near this woman. As though she were his homecoming and they belonged together. An odd notion, but there it was.

"Howdy." He waved, trying to sound casual. As though this meeting was a regular occurrence. No big deal. And he hoped she didn't notice the happy zing that seemed to fill his voice.

"Hi."

Jill's reply didn't sound too eager and he couldn't blame her. His profession and the question of timber theft hung between them like a thick iron curtain.

Without asking permission, Evie tightened

her fingers around the woman's hand. Showing complete trust. Assuming Jill would let her do it. And Jill did, looking completely unruffled by Evie's forward gesture.

Jill bent her knees so she could stoop down and meet the girl's eyes. "Have you been doing okay since I saw you last?"

Evie nodded, her long ponytail bouncing. Seeing his daughter so energized pleased Brent enormously. He didn't understand what it was about Jill that drew both him and Evie like a heat-seeking missile.

Jill smiled. "Good. I was planning to come and visit you later this evening. I have something for you in my car. I picked it up at the store before I drove up on the mountain. Would you like to see what it is?"

Another nod and bright, earnest eyes from the child. Brent hadn't seen Evie this engaged in a long time, and he marveled that Jill had this effect on his daughter.

Still holding Evie's hand, Jill walked with the girl toward her car. It was parked on the other side of the draw, hidden by a low-lying hill. No wonder Brent hadn't seen it when he'd first arrived.

Feeling a bit out of place, he trailed behind, curious to see Jill's surprise. At her car, she opened the back door and leaned inside.

The rustling of a plastic bag sounded as she pulled out a small dry-erase board. It included a miniature eraser with a magnet and a purple marker. Very interesting.

"Since you're now a big six-year-old, you're starting to learn to write, aren't you?" Jill asked.

Evie nodded with uncertainty, her gaze riveted on the erase board like it was Christmas morning.

"You can use this to write what you want to say and show it to your dad and other people. You can talk to him and anyone else that way. You want to try it?" Jill held out the board.

Evie didn't take it. A small shudder swept her body and she looked down at the ground.

Jill knelt in the dust, seeking Evie's gaze. When she spoke, her voice sounded infinitely gentle. "Don't worry if you don't know how to write well. That will come with time. If you can't spell a word, just draw a picture instead. Your dad will understand. The important thing is to keep trying. Don't ever give up. Do you think you can do that?"

Evie lifted her head and gave a tentative nod. Then, she reached out her hand and took the board. Jill showed her how to use the marker and eraser.

"Be sure to put the cap back on the eraser

right after you use it, or it'll dry out. Can you do that?" Jill asked.

Evie nodded. And that's when Brent noticed Jill always asked his daughter *yes* or *no* questions. Nothing complicated. Nothing that would make Evie feel overwhelmed and want to hide. Just simple queries that Evie could nod or shake her head on.

"Shall we try it out?" Jill stood straight.

Evie bobbed her head twice.

"Okay, do you like flowers and butterflies?"

Evie stared at the woman.

Jill pressed the tip of her finger against the board. "Just write yes or no."

Long seconds ticked by as it took Evie time to write her response, but Jill didn't rush her. Not one bit. And during that time, Brent held his breath. What if Evie refused to try? He wasn't sure if she knew how to spell the words. She'd refused to write at school. Her kindergarten teacher didn't think she knew how. And Brent assumed Evie wasn't learning a thing. He feared she'd grow up illiterate.

The black marker squeaked as Evie wrote some wobbly letters.

Yes.

Brent blinked his eyes, his throat feeling suddenly thick with emotion. His daughter could write. And if she could write, then that meant she could also read. At least a little. Obviously, Evie knew more than her teachers realized. And he had Jill to thank for revealing that fact.

Jill smiled. "Good. How about big black bears? Do you like them?"

They waited for Evie to write. It took less time for her to write the word *no*.

"That's okay. They can be kind of scary sometimes, right?"

Evie nodded.

"But I doubt any bears live in this empty forest." Jill's gaze lifted to the graveyard of trees, some of the stumps over three feet across.

Brent stared at her, entranced by the flicker of sunlight against her shiny hair. Thinking how she lit up the ugly forest with her beauty.

"Yeah, it's pretty sad," Brent agreed, forcing himself to look away. "But it'll recover. Clearing the tall trees from overhead opens up the plant life below to lots of sunlight. There won't be many trees in this area next summer, but the pine grass, currants and forbs will soon cover the ground with lots of vegetation. It'll take decades for the trees to come back, unless we help it out by replanting."

Evie stepped a short ways away, drawing a picture on her erase board.

"What do you estimate the dollar price of the theft is at?" Jill asked.

He pursed his lips, making some mental calculations. Grateful to have his attention drawn away from Jill's creamy complexion and the warm feelings coursing through his chest. "At least two hundred thousand dollars, possibly more."

Jill nodded. "I concur."

He wasn't surprised. She'd grown up in the timber business and knew the value of trees as well as he did.

Just then, she turned and stumbled over a low tree stump. He reached forward and caught her. She fell against him, one hand latching on to his biceps, the other sliding against his chest. She looked up and their eyes locked. He stared at her, mesmerized. For several pounding moments, they stood frozen in time. The world spun away and nothing existed but them. He felt her warmth and breathed in her fragrant scent. Her lips parted in surprise and he felt the overpowering urge to pull her in and kiss her.

Then he came to his senses. He must be losing his mind. He had to break this off right now. "You okay?"

She snapped back and blinked, not meeting his eyes. She brushed at her shirt, as though it was wrinkled. "Yes, I'm fine."

Think. What should he say? Something to appear normal and unaffected. To regain his composure.

"I…I've already started a replanting program to repair the damage to the forest," he said. "The crew should finish the work in another week or so, before the heat of summer comes in."

There. That was good. Right back to business.

She took a steadying breath. "I'd like to help."

He glanced at her, his eyes widening with wonder. "Seriously?"

"Yes."

"Why?"

She blinked, as though his blunt question had taken her off guard. And quite frankly, he was feeling a bit off balance himself. He didn't understand how a woman could smell so delectable.

"Do I need a reason?" she asked.

"No, it's just that I didn't expect you to help with the project. Under the circumstances, I think you can understand my surprise."

"Yes, you're right," she conceded. "It doesn't make sense to me either. But I'd really like to help. It's for a great cause. I want to ensure our forests stay forested and there are trees to harvest in the future. Mankind has done enough damage to our earth already. So, when do you need me?"

He looked away, thinking. "Um, I've got a work crew planning to come out again next Monday morning. They'll be finished with their work by noon. So you've got a few days. If you come to the Forest Service office, you can ride up with them and know exactly where they'll be working."

"Okay, what time?" He told her the necessary information and she nodded her acceptance. "I'll be there, so don't let them leave without me. I want to work with the Forest Service in any way I can to clear my brother's name. He insists he didn't have any part in this theft, and I believe him. So we're eager to help catch whoever did this and clear our name."

Our name. He couldn't help noticing that she included herself with her brother. And although he was positive she was completely innocent of any wrongdoing in the situation, her loyalty to her family was just one more reason he liked her.

"I'm glad to hear that. But like I said, we haven't made any accusations yet." He shifted his weight, again wishing he could confide in her. Wishing he didn't have to keep the truth a secret. It was a good thing Alan hadn't betrayed his instructions from the US Attorney's office.

She showed a skeptical smile. The silence lengthened and he knew what she was thinking. Soon enough, the LEI would want to prowl around her family's sawmill as they performed an investigation. It was inevitable. Having Jill's cooperation would help a great deal with the ugly chore.

A tug on his arm brought his head down to Evie. She held up her erase board and he saw that she'd written the word *danc*. She'd drawn a little stick figure at the side, wearing what appeared to be a ballerina tutu. She then pointed at Jill.

He crinkled his brow. "Do you mean *dance*?"

Evie nodded and jabbed her finger more forcefully toward Jill.

"You want to invite Jill to your dance recital?" he asked.

A bright smile lit up Evie's face and she pumped her head up and down. Brent tried not to stare, but it'd been so long since he'd been able to communicate effectively with her. And seeing her smile again knocked the breath right out of him.

His gaze swung back to Jill. "Um, Evie would like to invite you to her dance recital tomorrow night. It's at seven, in the civic center."

Okay, he'd made the invitation. From the withdrawn expression on Jill's face, he could tell she felt uncomfortable about it, too. It didn't help that she'd tripped and he'd held her in his arms like a giant leech.

Jill bent at the waist and smiled at Evie. "I'd love to come, sweetheart, but I've already got a commitment with my own family. I'll try to make it if I can. Okay?"

The woman was trying to be so careful. So considerate. Trying not to injure Evie's feelings. And Brent appreciated her efforts more than he could say.

Evie nodded, but didn't hide her disappointment. She sidled over to Brent and took his hand as she stared at the ground in dejection.

"Ah, we're still friends, aren't we?" Jill asked, her voice filled with invitation.

Evie glanced at her, then gave a timid smile indicating they were.

"Good." Jill stepped back. "Well, I've got to get back to work. Nice to see you both again."

"Yeah. You, too," Brent said.

He breathed an audible sigh of relief when she got into her car, turned on the engine and headed down the dirt road.

Watching her go, he missed her already. And he shouldn't miss this woman. She was nothing to him. Just a permittee whose sawmill cut logs on national forest lands. And yet, he couldn't fight the bevy of mixed emotions in his mind. How he wished they'd met under different circumstances. How he regretted that the timber-theft issue stood between them like a huge dangerous giant.

Maybe it was best if Jill didn't attend Evie's dance program tomorrow evening. Because his heart and mind couldn't take the emotional assault.

Chapter Four

Brent awoke slowly. The sounds of voices drifted in and out of his mind. He was dreaming. Yet, it seemed so real.

No, it wasn't a dream.

He blinked his eyes. The sounds filtered around him. Voices sifting through the house in hushed tones. Subtle but persistent.

He sprang into a sitting position and stared into the dark. A quick glance at the electronic clock resting on the bedside table told him it was one thirty-eight in the morning. He'd been asleep for less than an hour.

Everything looked normal. Night shadows clung to the large dresser hugging the far wall. The basket of clean laundry sat right where he'd abandoned it earlier, still waiting to be folded and put away. He'd been too tired to deal with it before morning.

For a few moments, the voices faded. He heard nothing. Just the hum of crickets outside his bedroom window and the persistent whoosh of the furnace blowing warm air throughout the house. Maybe the neighbors were getting in late. Maybe they were watching a late-night show and had the TV volume turned up too high. Maybe he'd imagined the noise.

He shifted his weight against the mattress, prepared to lie down and go back to sleep.

There it was again! The unmistakable sounds of people talking. It wasn't the neighbors. It was here in his house. And in a rush, he realized what must be happening.

Evie couldn't sleep. Again.

Tossing aside the blanket, he swung his legs over the side of the bed and stood. Padding barefoot across the thick Berber carpet, he paused in the hallway and cocked his head to one side, listening.

Yes, definitely the TV set in his living room. Treading down the hall, he peeked around the corner. All the lights were off; an eerie red glow emanated from the TV screen. Evie lay curled on the couch, snuggled beneath her monkey blankie. Lina had made the blanket when Evie was a newborn baby. Evie had later named it after the myriad of little blue monkeys covering the soft flannel. It was one of her most prized possessions. A memory of her mother. The girl never went to bed without it and her stuffed bunny rabbit. Both the bunny and the blanket were now so threadbare that Brent didn't dare wash them anymore. They might fall apart, and he feared he wouldn't be able to console Evie over their loss.

She wasn't asleep. She stared into the dark room, her eyes wide open and trained on the TV. The shopping channel, thank goodness. The variety of late-night shows were for adults, not an innocent little girl who couldn't sleep. TV was a Band-Aid for a much bigger problem he didn't know how to fix.

He leaned against the doorjamb. His movements must have caught Evie's attention. In one movement, her gaze shifted to him, her chin went up, her eyes flared and she cringed.

Terrorized.

"It's okay, sweetheart. It's just me," he said soothingly.

Recognizing her daddy, she relaxed, her tiny fingers clutching folds of the monkey blankie up against her neck. In spite of the warm air, her slender shoulders shivered noticeably. He walked to her and sat down, pulling her onto his lap. She coiled against his chest, her cheek pressed against his heart. A huge sigh escaped her lips, as though she were relieved he was there.

He kissed her hair, catching the fruity scent of shampoo from her evening bath. "Can't you sleep, honey?"

He felt her shake her head.

"Did you have another nightmare?" He rested his chin against her forehead.

Another shake *no*.

He took a deep inhale and let it go. "Are you afraid to go to sleep?"

A nod *yes*.

"Why, sweetheart? We're here in our own home, safe and sound. No one is going to hurt you here. I won't let them."

He looked down at her face and caught her mournful expression. So lost. So afraid.

She didn't answer, but he didn't really expect her to. Sometimes he missed her sweet voice. Missed her bright laughter, too. It was so hard having a one-sided conversation with his own daughter. Trying to figure out what was wrong, or what she wanted, or how to help her. He thought about asking where she'd put the dry-erase board. But no. That would require turning on lights and searching the entire house. And right now, he wanted her to calm down and go to sleep.

"Are you afraid you might have a nightmare?" he asked.

A small shudder swept her body and she nodded *yes*. Brent's heart gave a powerful squeeze. How he ached for her anguish.

He blinked his eyes, wondering what to do. When she had a nightmare, she usually woke up screaming. But tonight, she was too afraid to sleep. Fearful of closing her eyes for what might lurk behind her imagination.

"It's okay. I'm here now. You can rest. I promise not to leave you."

He hoped that one day she'd recover from her fears. That she'd start talking again and they'd live a normal, happy life.

He almost snorted. Happy? He didn't know what that meant anymore. He'd been happy before Lina was killed. He'd had the world in the palm of his hands. A challenging career. A beautiful, loving wife. A sweet little daughter. What more could a man ask for? And in the blink of an eye, it was taken from him. He didn't even get to tell Lina goodbye. Not until he'd seen her in the morgue. And then, he'd wept for hours afterward. Great wrenching sobs. Because he knew all that he'd lost. And he knew Evie would have to grow up without her mommy.

For now, he lay back against the couch,

tucking her monkey blankie around her spindly legs. She didn't sleep. Not for a very long time. She snuggled her arms against his chest, her hands clutching folds of his nightshirt as though that would hold him there like a lifeline. He could feel her body tensed against him, constricted with fear.

For several hours, Brent sat there and dozed. Ever conscious of his daughter, he'd awaken with a jerk and glanced down at her face. She blinked up at him, her chin tightening. Without saying so, he knew she feared he might tuck her back into her bed. Alone. With her nightmares.

But he wouldn't. Not when it might traumatize her more. He hadn't been there for her when Lina was killed and he wouldn't abandon her now.

Around five o'clock, he caught the first rays of sunlight filtering through the window curtains. He felt Evie relax against him and heard her soft, even breathing. Her long lashes curved against her smooth cheeks, her mouth slightly open. In that moment, she looked so much like her mother that his throat constricted in a wave of grief. He knew one thing for sure. Until Evie recovered, she needed his full attention.

He thought about Jill Russell and her gentle way of handling his daughter.

He pushed such thoughts aside. It did no good to torture himself. This was reality and he had to deal with it. But he and Evie couldn't continue like this. He'd tried everything he could think of, but nothing had worked. It was time to take action. He prayed silently, asking for help. Asking how to get Evie to accept that she was safe. That no harm would come to her.

Ask Jill Russell for help.

The thought popped into his mind with perfect clarity, but he shook his head. He couldn't call on Jill. No doubt her entire family resented him. Yet what other options did he have left? He'd do anything for his daughter. Even ask Jill, if he thought she'd help. But she wouldn't. He was almost certain of it.

Or would she? He'd never know unless he asked.

On Thursday night, Jill pulled her car into the parking lot at the civic center. Late again. Dinner with her mom and brother had kept her overlong. Ellen, her old friend from high school, had called to invite her to attend her daughter's dance recital, or she wouldn't have come here at all. Not when it meant running into Brent again.

The glow from the streetlights gleamed overhead as she found a parking place far away from the entrance and killed the engine. She snatched up her purse and threw open the door. Rushing up the front walkway, she stepped into the white brick building and hurried toward the cultural hall.

She must be crazy. What was she doing here? She had no idea. It wasn't so she could see Evie and Brent again. No, she'd come to see Ellen, her best friend from high school. As teenagers, they'd been inseparable. Until Jill left for college and Ellen married her high school sweetheart and remained here in Bartlett to raise her three kids.

Ellen's daughter, Chrissy, was Evie's age. That's why Jill was here. To be supportive of her friends. To watch Chrissy perform. Or at least that's what Jill told herself.

She stepped inside the outer foyer. Over the loudspeaker, someone's voice announced the first number. Great! She hadn't missed anything. Just in time.

As she made her way into the dimly lit hall, she blinked to adjust her vision. She sidled her way down the narrow aisle, looking for a vacant seat. The place was jam-packed with gawking parents. She moved toward the front, thinking she might have to crouch at the foot of the stage to watch Evie dance.

Correction. To see Chrissy dance. But Jill didn't mind being here for Evie, too. After all, it was important not to let the little girl down. Evie had invited Jill and she was happy to give the child some support. The girl had been through a lot. She deserved so much more. But a niggling doubt at the back of Jill's mind asked her why she cared so much.

Spying an empty seat, she ducked her head and went for it, climbing over people to get there before the program began. Grace Harvey, one of her mother's friends, glared with disapproval as she stepped past the woman's feet.

"You're late," Grace whispered in a low hiss.

Tossing the woman an apologetic smile, Jill kept going.

Cal Winfield, a worker at the sawmill, waved as she hurdled his long legs, trying not to break her own ankle in the process. She gave him a lame smile.

As she sat down, Susan Winfield patted her arm and whispered. "It's good to see you again. You in town for long?"

"Just a few weeks," Jill claimed, hoping it was true. But after what she'd seen at the sawmill, she feared she'd be here all summer long.

The woman nodded and focused on the

stage. Jill looked up and swallowed hard. Brent Knowles had turned in his seat and looked at her. She took in his angular face and the sparkle in his dazzling blue eyes. She remembercd when she'd tripped and latched on to him to keep from falling flat on her face. For several long moments, she'd found herself spellbound by him. So handsome that she'd had to swallow hard.

He sat one row ahead and two seats to the left. So close that she could almost reach out and touch him. She'd hoped to avoid him tonight but realized that was impossible now.

She returned his half smile and looked away, feeling suddenly flustered and self-conscious. She didn't understand this attraction between them. Hopefully, Brent would turn around and ignore her. Maybe she shouldn't have come tonight. She'd felt compelled, as though her future happiness depended on it. A weird notion, if ever she'd had one.

Staring at the stage, she folded her arms and took a deep, settling breath. But it didn't help much. She could almost feel Brent's gaze resting on her like a load of bricks. And the worst part about it was that she longed to talk to him. About nothing and everything. To say hello and ask how Evie was doing. To discuss her concerns about the sawmill's financial situation. To ask about the timber theft. And why she had the urge to confide in Brent Knowles, she had no idea. He was a stranger. An outsider. And she shouldn't trust him one bit.

Scratchy music filtered over the air. As if on cue, a line of adorable little girls, ages five to six years, filed past the front row of spectators. Each girl wore a pink tutu, matching leotards and black tap shoes. The fifth child in the row was Chrissy, immediately followed by Evie. Their long blond hair had been pulled up in a bun on top of their heads with a gangly pink flower pinned at the side. Sweet and cute as buttons. All of the tiny girls looked identical, except that Evie didn't smile.

The kids swung their arms as they tromped up the steps and onto the stage. Instead of delicate ballerinas, they sounded like a herd of cattle. A low murmur of delighted laughter filtered over the audience.

The lead dancer scurried across the stage in a fast trot with the other girls following behind. When the first girl stopped abruptly at the end of the stage, the second girl plowed straight into her back. This set off a chain reaction of dominoes with the girls sequentially butting against each other. It took several more moments for the children to regain their balance and adjust their spacing.

The parents in the audience chuckled and clapped with pleasure. Jill stole a quick glance at Brent. His chiseled profile softened with his wide grin. Like any proud father, he appeared to be completely enjoying himself.

Jill forced herself to look away and smiled so hard that it hurt her face. And when the music started and the girls began to tap-dance, she laughed out loud.

The miniature ballerinas tried to snap their fingers in time to the awkward clicking of their feet. Since they were so young and still trying to gain their coordination, most of them could do no more than rub their thumbs and index fingers together. Each child was off-beat, their timing wrong, but that didn't stop them from twirling and swaying their arms. And it didn't matter one bit to the audience. These little girls were so endearing that Jill's heart melted at the cuteness of it all. And right then and there, she couldn't help feeling deep and abiding regret that none of the girls belonged to her. That she might never know the joys of being a wife and mother.

Brent's deep laugh sifted through the air as he clapped his approval. How she wished she could have met and married a man like him. How she envied the love he'd shared with his wife and daughter. Jill would give almost anything to be cherished like that. She'd always wanted children, but David hated kids. He'd claimed they were too messy, cost too much money and took up too much time. Selfish reasons not to have any of his own. A number of times during their marriage, Jill had thought of tricking him into becoming a father, but she didn't want to base their marriage on lies. In retrospect, she was glad they'd never had kids. But that didn't keep her from wanting them. Now she might never get another chance to have a family of her own. And sitting among a plethora of friends and neighbors she'd known her entire life, she felt more alone than ever before.

The tempo of the music changed and Jill shook off her morose mood. Evie spiraled and stopped dead, staring straight at Jill. Lifting a hand, Jill gave a tentative wave. A wide, angelic smile broke out across Evie's face. So sudden, that Jill knew it was a rare occurrence. And from her peripheral vision, Jill caught the glance of Brent looking her way. But other people were staring at her, too.

Taken off guard, the dancer behind Evie smacked right into her. Evie jerked around in surprise, her smile replaced by a scowl of irritation. Momentarily distracted, the two children pushed against each other, which upset the other dancers. They crowded close, taking sides. Before the dance dissolved into a brawl, Susan Galloway, the instructor, scurried up the steps and sped across the stage to break it up.

Low laughter swept across the audience. People were staring at Jill. She recognized everyone. Employees from the sawmill. The grocery store owner. Her mother's cronies from church. People she'd gone to school with. Jill figured almost the entire town was here tonight. And as her face heated up like road flares, she felt as though every one of them was gawking at her.

Brent looked over his shoulder, his gaze latching on to Jill. She expected him to throw her a frown of disapproval. Instead, he grinned. Of course the people sitting beside her noticed. Their gazes immediately flashed back and forth between them. And Jill knew what that meant. In small towns, gossip traveled fast. No doubt they'd all be discussing this unexpected turn of events as soon as the recital ended. Some wouldn't care. Others who earned their living with logging wouldn't approve. No, not at all. True or false, they'd deduce that the sawmill owner was conspiring with the ranger.

She slunk lower in her seat, wishing she hadn't waved at Evie. And yet, she figured the girl needed a friend now more than ever. Someone she could look up to. Someone she could trust. But Jill wished it didn't have to be her.

Wasn't Brent bothered by all the people staring at them? Didn't he feel the disapproval in their eyes? Surely he cared what others thought. But maybe not. And she envied his self-confidence.

Releasing a low groan, Jill ducked her head and wished she could disappear into thin air. If only she hadn't come here tonight. She wished she didn't care what other people thought about her, but she did. And yet, maybe she should change that. Maybe she should simply do what she thought was right.

With a semblance of order restored, the little girls finished their number with a flourish of arms and bobbing heads. The audience cheered with applause. Susan led the children off stage, her face tight with a severe frown. If she didn't realize it yet, Jill figured someone would soon tell the instructor what had caused the uproar and nearly ruined her students' performance.

At that moment, Jill figured she had a choice. She could stay for the rest of the program and face Evie and her father in the chaotic aftermath, or she could flee. Right now. Before anyone could stop her.

But braving more angry glares as she sidled past everyone in her aisle to make a hasty retreat didn't appeal to Jill either.

She stayed. But the remainder of the recital was pure torture. Watching the plethora of girls and one boy dance was great, but Jill didn't want to give the town any more fodder for gossip. It was bad enough that most of them already knew about her divorce and that her ex had cheated on her. She felt ugly and unworthy to be around anyone right now. In fact, it was downright humiliating.

She tightened her fists in her lap. The moment the program ended, she popped out of her seat and pushed her way past the people in her row. Almost there.

Until she came face-to-face with Brent. He stood in her path, blocking her way to freedom.

"Hi, Jill." He smiled, his eyes twinkling.

Heaven help her, she smiled back. "Um, hi."

In the clogged aisle, someone bumped against her back, propelling her forward. To stop herself, she lifted her hands and pressed her palms against Brent's solid chest. Her cheek bumped against the soft fabric of his navy shirt. He smelled delectable. Like sandalwood. And she took a deep inhale, wanting more.

He clasped her shoulders, holding her upright. A ripple of muscles moved beneath her fingertips. Her head felt suddenly woozy, as though she were going to faint.

"You okay?" he asked.

She looked up, spellbound by his translucent blue eyes. He'd slicked his hair back, his chin freshly shaven. She almost reached up to caress his smooth cheek, which would be absolutely catastrophic right now. She couldn't understand why she'd become such a klutz around him. If she wasn't careful, he might get the wrong idea and think she was flirting with him.

Someone coughed nearby and she snapped back, hoping no one else noticed. Trying to gain control over her sensibilities.

"Yes, I'm fine. It's just a bit crowded in here," she mumbled.

"It is. Come on." He took her hand, guiding her through the horde of people to the front foyer where they had more room to move.

With his warm fingers wrapped around hers, she had no choice but to follow. With his tall height clearing the way, everyone stepped out of their way. He commanded attention, controlling the situation without saying a word. In all her life, she'd never been so glad to trail behind someone. Clinging to his hand, she ducked her head, her cheeks blazing with heat. Currents of electricity zipped up her arm where her skin made contact with his. To avoid being rude, she didn't pull away. Right now, she didn't know if she should view him as her champion, or the source of her problems.

Maybe both.

It seemed hours before he released her. He'd taken her to the main foyer where long tables had been set up with white plastic tablecloths and trays of cookies. She stood beside the punch bowl accepting a paper cup he pressed into her hands. Taking a sip of red punch, she felt dazed and silly all at once. She had no idea why this man's presence made her so nervous, or why she cared what other people thought about her. She had her life in Boise and wouldn't be here very long. None of this mattered.

Unless someone tattled to her mother.

"Thanks for coming to Evie's recital. It means a lot to her," he said.

But why? Jill couldn't understand the immediate attachment between her and Evie. Probably because she was a special-ed teacher and trained to help. To care. But why had Evie taken such a liking to her? It didn't make sense.

"I…I also came to see Chrissy, my best friend's daughter." That was true, but it sounded lame to her ears. She just couldn't stand for Brent to think she was here to see him.

"Who's your friend?" he asked.

He leaned close enough for her to take another deep inhale of his masculine scent.

"Ellen Davinger. She's married to Mike Davinger. Do you know them?"

He chuckled, his gaze scanning the crowd of people as they congregated in the foyer for refreshments. "I do, as a matter of fact. Chrissy's come over to our house to play a few times. She doesn't mind Evie's silence and they've become good friends, although I've never been able to coax Evie into going over to Chrissy's house without me tagging along."

In this small town, Jill wasn't surprised they were friends. Ellen rarely found fault with anyone, which was why Jill loved her so much. And Mike worked for the state road crews, so his livelihood wasn't associated with the lumber business and its bias against the Forest Service. Mike could afford to let his children associate with the forest ranger's daughter without adverse consequences falling back on his head.

"Evie was awfully cute in her performance tonight," Jill murmured.

He laughed, the deep sound of rolling thunder. "Yeah, she definitely has a penchant for cuteness. It's one of her specialties. But I think all the kids did a great job tonight."

Fred Baker, a logger from the sawmill, stepped between them and reached for a peanut butter cookie. His gaze ricocheted off Jill and then Brent. His eyes darkened and his mouth tightened with disapproval as he turned and tromped away.

Glancing over her shoulder, Jill saw other people staring at her, their heads bent close together as they discussed what she was doing fraternizing with the local forest ranger.

"Um, I better get going." Jill took a step back, prepared to run for her car the moment she hit the outer door.

Brent touched her arm with his fingertips and she fought off a shiver of excitement. "Actually, before you go, I was hoping to ask if you might be willing to…"

A tug on Jill's hand pulled her around.

"Evie!"

The girl still wore her pink tutu and tap shoes, an expectant smile on her face.

"You did so well tonight. I can tell you've practiced really hard." Jill's voice sounded unusually high and jittery.

The girl's smile deepened into pure bliss. Jill couldn't fathom why her approval meant so much to the child. But heaven help her, it made her care even more.

Brent gave Evie a tight hug. "Hi, sweetheart. You did well tonight. It was a great performance. I'm so proud of you."

Evie cast a shy glance at the floor, beaming with satisfaction. From her open body language, Jill could tell his praise pleased her. And from the standpoint of a special-ed teacher trying to help a student overcome a traumatic event, Jill believed this was great progress in increasing Evie's self-confidence.

Ida Parker, the office manager at the mill, brushed past. When she caught sight of Jill talking with Brent, she turned in open surprise. "Jill! What are you doing here?"

The woman's shrewd gaze darted between her, Brent and Evie. Jill almost groaned out loud. She could almost see the wheels turning in Ida's head as she made her own deductions.

So much for Mom not finding out.

"I was attending the dance recital, of course. Ellen's little girl was performing tonight. I'm just being supportive." It was a lame excuse, but it should work.

"Ellen and Chrissy are way over there." Ida pointed across the room.

The hackles lifted at the back of Jill's neck. She didn't like being told what to do, especially by a mill employee. But she also realized she was bypassing the order of things by speaking socially to Brent.

Jill spotted Ellen headed in her direction. So much for making a quick getaway. She would have preferred to visit Ellen tomorrow, but since she had called Jill earlier to invite her to Chrissy's recital, she had no option but to say hello.

Seeming to understand Jill's predicament, Brent took Evie's hand and tugged her away. "Thanks again. We'll say good-night, now."

"Hi, sweetie. Oh, I've missed you." Ellen gave Jill a tight hug.

"Hi, there." Jill pasted a plastic smile on her face. Normally, she would have loved to catch up with her friend. But not right now. Not with so many other people staring at her with judgmental eyes.

"Thanks again for inviting me, Ellen— Chrissy was great." She moved in a little closer and whispered to her friend, "Listen, I'd love to chat, but can we do it tomorrow?"

Ellen glanced at Brent, who was encouraging Evie to go into the dressing room and change her clothes. Ellen nodded, seeming to understand Jill's discomfort. "I'll come over to your mom's house in the morning."

"Sounds good." Jill nodded and headed off,

wishing she'd never come here in the first place. Wishing she'd never met Brent Knowles and his cute little girl. Because now, she felt invested in Evie. She cared about the little girl, she couldn't deny it. And if ever there was a time in her life when she didn't need more complications to deal with, this was it.

Chapter Five

Bright sunlight streamed through the kitchen window. With a quick twist of her wrist, Jill reached up and flipped the blind open wide. She took a deep inhale, enjoying the sudden warmth. It had rained last night, leaving behind a fragrant scent of washed earth and sage. Reaching inside the refrigerator, she pulled out a pitcher of homemade lemonade.

"So, what's up with you and the forest ranger?"

Jill whipped her head around and stared at Ellen, who sat at the table, bouncing her ten-month-old baby, Tommy, on her knee. Ellen had come over for a visit and the two women had been chatting and catching up for the past ten minutes.

"What do you mean?" Jill's hands became

shaky all of a sudden and she tightened her grip on the glass pitcher as she shut the fridge door.

Ellen showed an impish smile. "I saw the way you two were looking at each other last night. You like him, and he likes you."

"I have no idea what you're talking about. I already told you how I first met him and Evie. When we see each other, it's normal for us to say hello. It's nothing more than that. He's the forest ranger, after all." Jill set the pitcher on the counter and reached for two glasses. She hid her scalding face behind the cupboard door, telling herself she had nothing to be embarrassed about. There was nothing between her and Brent Knowles. So why did she feel as though there was?

Ellen shook her head. "I'm glad you were there to help Evie that day at the gas station. She's such a sweet little thing. She must be missing her mommy an awful lot. To actually see her mother get killed, it's no wonder the girl won't speak a word."

"Yeah, the situation must be difficult for both her and Brent. I honestly don't know how they're doing as well as they are. It says a lot about Brent that he hasn't given up on Evie," Jill said.

"Yes, from what I've observed, he's a man

with loyal principles. Unlike that snake in the grass you recently divorced."

Jill's mouth dropped open as she thought of a rebuttal. She wanted to defend David but couldn't. Not if she were being honest with herself. He didn't deserve it.

"But you sure were chummy with Brent last night," Ellen continued with a lift of her brows. "You sure you're not attracted to him?"

Jill shrugged, trying to act casual. Trying to ignore the pounding of her heart. Of course she found him attractive. She'd have to be dead not to. "I'm recently divorced."

"And what's that got to do with Brent?"

"I'm not interested in any man. We were just discussing the dance recital. No big deal. We're acquaintances, nothing more."

Jill poured the lemonade and carried the glasses to the table, setting one in front of her friend. Ellen reached for a chocolate chip cookie and broke off a tiny piece for Tommy. With only two teeth, the baby gummed the cookie happily.

As she slid into her seat, Jill felt Ellen's gaze resting on her like a ten-ton sledge. To hide her discomposure, Jill reached for her glass and took a sip. It went down the wrong pipe and she coughed.

"You okay?" Ellen wrapped an arm around

the baby, as though preparing to stand and help Jill by pounding her on the back.

"Yes," Jill gasped. She took another drink, swallowed and settled into her chair.

"It's time you moved past David. You should go out with Brent. He's a nice man and has morals. He wouldn't hurt you the way David did," Ellen said.

Jill coughed again, not out of necessity, but in an effort to divert her friend off this topic. Having grown up in Bartlett, Ellen was highly aware of the animosity that existed between loggers and Forest Service employees. Suggesting that Jill date the man was ludicrous.

"Sorry, but that's not gonna happen." Jill spoke in a mild tone. She decided not to get upset by this topic. After all, Brent had no interest in her and she doubted he'd ever ask her out anyway.

"No, I mean it. From what I've seen, he'd be perfect for you. Not like that weasel you divorced. What does Brent's profession matter? You've both been through a lot. And you both deserve some happiness." Ellen offered the rim of her glass to Tommy and wasn't looking when Jill threw her a dark glare. Ellen held tight to make sure the baby didn't spill as he joyfully sucked in mouthfuls of the sweet lemonade.

"Thanks, but I doubt the ranger is interested

in one of the sawmill owners. And I guarantee I'm not interested in him, or any man for that matter. For the time being, I like being single."

Ellen smiled. "Well, you both looked interested last night."

"How would you know?" Jill challenged.

The baby gurgled and waved his chubby arms. Jill reached across the table and let him grip one of her fingers as she focused on his drooling smile. Talking about her failed marriage and dating other men made her feel strangely lost and undeserving. All her friends were married with children, and she couldn't help thinking she'd never have a sweet little baby of her own to love.

"A girl just knows these things. If you weren't still recovering from the divorce, you would have noticed Brent, too. A man doesn't pay that kind of attention to a woman he doesn't like."

Shaking her head, Jill took another swallow of lemonade. "He was just being nice."

"Oh, phooey. You're gorgeous and so is he. In fact, you're perfect for each other."

"Perfect? Obviously you've forgotten what he does for a living. We're worlds apart. Besides, my family would never approve."

The doorbell rang. Down the hall, Arline

Russell came out of her bedroom and made a beeline for the living room.

"I'll get it, girls. You two continue with your visit," she trilled as she passed by the kitchen.

"Your mom seems happy today," Ellen said.

"Yes, she's been like that since I got home. I think she's been lonely since Dad died. And she's worried about Alan, too."

"Well, I'm worried about you. Why don't you call him?"

"Who?"

Ellen snorted. "Brent Knowles, that's who."

"Shh," Jill shushed her friend and whispered low. "I don't want Mom to overhear us talking about him. It would only upset her more. Besides, I already told you I'm not interested."

"Yeah, sure. I believe you. And pigs can fly." Ellen laughed.

"Jill?"

She looked up and flinched. Mom stood in the doorway, but she wasn't smiling. Her forehead was creased in a severe scowl. A woman of fifty-six years of age, her normally rosy cheeks looked ashen, her eyes narrowed in an angry scowl.

"What's up?" Jill asked, feeling guilty for even discussing the ranger inside Mom's house.

"The forest ranger is here to see you." Mom

growled the words, her happy mood evaporating like drops of water on hot cement.

Jill's mouth fell open. Conscious of Ellen's eyes widening in surprise, she didn't know what to say.

"What's he doing here?" Mom hissed.

"I…I have no idea," Jill answered truthfully.

"Well, I don't want that man in my house. Get rid of him." Rather than returning to the living room to welcome their guest, Mom turned with an angry huff and stomped down the hallway to her bedroom. A moment later, the door slammed to mark her passing.

Oh, this wasn't good. Unless Brent was bringing some news about the timber-theft case. Which Jill doubted. Not yet, anyway.

Jill knew her mom would remain sequestered until the ranger left the house. And then, Jill would have some explaining to do.

"Uh-huh. I can see there's nothing going on between you two." Ellen cast a sly glance at Jill before pushing back her chair and reaching down to pick up her diaper bag.

Jill inwardly groaned and closed her eyes for the count of three. Right now, she wanted to crawl in a hole and hide somewhere. After she'd emphatically denied there was anything going on between her and Brent, he then had the audacity to show up at her mother's house and make it appear that Jill was hiding something. And she wasn't. She was going back to Boise at the end of the summer. End of story.

Or was it?

"I better see what he wants," Jill murmured.

She walked into the living room, conscious of Ellen following right behind her with Tommy balanced against her hip. The woman grinned when she caught sight of Brent still standing in the open doorway. Drafts of chilly spring air flooded the room. Mom obviously hadn't invited him inside.

As she met his gorgeous blue eyes, Jill's mouth went dry, her palms damp. She couldn't take an even breath. A warning tingle slid down the column of her spine. All her senses ratcheted into high alert. Her mind buzzed. Common sense told her it was too soon for him to bring her news of the timber issue. The LEI agent wasn't coming in until sometime next week. So what was Brent doing here?

"Hi, Brent," Ellen greeted him with warmth.

"Hello. I thought I saw your car parked out front." He showed an uncertain smile.

In spite of wearing his ranger uniform, complete with the brass shield pinned to the front of his shirt, he glanced at Jill with hesitancy. He shifted his booted feet, looking out of place.

Like he didn't want to be here any more than Mom wanted him here.

"Jill and I are old friends from high school. We were just catching up. Is Evie with you?" Ellen shifted Tommy to her other hip.

Brent reached out and offered his index finger to the baby, who latched on and chortled. "No, she's over at Mrs. Crawford's house. I'm going to pick her up as soon as I'm finished with my business here."

Jill listened with rapt attention. Velma Crawford was a friend of Mom's. Since Evie was the forest ranger's daughter, Jill was surprised Velma had agreed to watch the child. But Jill also knew Velma was a widow living on a tight budget. She undoubtedly needed the extra money. Besides, who wouldn't love Evie at first sight?

"I'm hoping you'll bring her over to my house to play with Chrissy soon," Ellen said.

"That would be nice, if I can get Evie to go. It's a battle just to get her to stay with Mrs. Crawford. I think she does it because she knows I have to go to work. She likes Mrs. Crawford okay, but she still doesn't feel completely at ease."

Jill understood. Evie probably didn't feel safe anywhere.

"Don't worry about it. She'll come over to

play at our house when she feels ready. In the meantime, I'm happy to bring Chrissy over to your house any time you want, or you can come over and visit with Mike while Evie plays with my kids," Ellen suggested.

He flashed that devastating smile of his and Jill blinked, feeling warm and tingly all over.

"I'd like that. You're very understanding of our situation. Maybe in time, Evie won't hesitate." He didn't sound too positive.

"Of course. Nothing's more important than our kids. I want to see Evie get better. If there's anything I can do to help, just name it." The diaper bag slipped down Ellen's arm and she gave a quick jerk, pulling the strap back over her shoulder.

Jill listened to this exchange with interest. What a lonely, isolated life both Brent and Evie must be living. This town was filled with people who didn't like them simply because of Brent's profession, not to mention Evie's handicap.

"Now, I'll leave you two alone," Ellen gushed.

Brent stepped aside to let her pass. Jill caught the tantalizing whiff of his spicy aftershave. In spite of the drab olive color of his ranger's shirt, he looked quite handsome in his uniform. Tall as a church steeple, with chiseled features that would make any woman stop for a second look. And thinking such thoughts caused her face to heat up like a flame thrower. Which brought another amused snicker from Ellen.

"Call me later, sweetie. We've still got a lot to talk about." Carrying Tommy with her, Ellen turned her back on Brent, waggled her eyebrows at Jill and flashed a suggestive smile.

Jill didn't say a word. She didn't dare. Instead, she bit her tongue, wanting to strangle her friend right now.

"I didn't mean to interrupt. I can come back later," Brent said.

"Absolutely not! I was just leaving. You stay as long as you like," Ellen encouraged him.

She slipped out the door and down the steps so fast that Jill couldn't have stopped her if she'd wanted to. And she didn't want to. Right now, she wanted to be left alone.

Brent jerked his thumb toward the vacant doorway. "She's a nice lady."

"Yes, and it's good for Evie to have at least one friend. Have a seat." Jill moved to close the door, shutting out the cold drafts of air.

He sat in a soft-backed chair, his long legs and wide shoulders stiff and unyielding. He rubbed his hands over his knees and gave a nervous laugh. "Maybe I should have called first before coming over."

She agreed, but thought it'd be rude to say so. She wanted to tell him it was all right for him to be here, but they both knew better. She liked this man and his sweet little girl, but she didn't want to. Not only because of who he was, but also because of what he made her feel. No matter what Ellen said, Jill doubted she'd ever trust another man again.

Out of her peripheral vision, she could see Brent watching her and felt singed by his gaze. Her brain cells liquefied, and she wondered what this man did to her senses. She hadn't just fallen off the turnip truck. She wasn't inter-ested in romance. At least, not until her heart stopped aching every time she thought about her failed marriage. But for some reason, there was a gravitational pull between her and Brent that she couldn't deny. Something she'd never felt before, not even with her ex-husband.

Trying to still the quaking of her knees, she sat across from him. She tucked her bare feet beneath her and released a deep sigh of resig-nation. "So, what did you want to speak with me about?"

Here it was. The big question. A huge whoosh of air escaped Brent's lungs as he sat forward and contemplated how to make his request. After facing Arline Russell's ugly glare, he knew he wasn't wanted here. To make matters worse, Jill sat across from him, watching him like a bug under a microscope.

"I came to ask if I can pay you to work with Evie. To help her get past her trauma and start speaking again." There! He'd said it. But maybe he shouldn't have blurted it out like that.

She quirked a brow in disbelief.

He hurried on, before she could say no. "I wouldn't ask if I wasn't desperate. You're the first person to get through to Evie. Even little Chrissy can't get her to talk. Evie's fine with the little girl, as long as I'm there with them. I've taken her to numerous specialists, but it's always the same. She won't talk. She won't do any schoolwork until she gets home with me. The only person she's ever reacted positively to is you. Something about you makes her happy. You make her feel safe."

Jill hugged a tasseled pillow to her chest and stared at him, her eyes filled with confusion or disbelief, he wasn't sure which.

"Do you realize what you're asking me to do?" she said.

"Yes, I'm asking you to help rescue my daughter." He spoke with conviction. If it was for himself, he never would have asked. But where Evie was concerned, he'd face a million forest-ranger haters, if it meant his daughter could be whole again.

Jill rubbed her chin briskly. A sure sign of exasperation. He expected her to say no and ask him to get out of her house and never come back. But then, she folded her arms across the pillow and looked down at the cream-colored carpet. Quiet and thoughtful.

He didn't speak. Didn't move or breathe. Afraid to upset her. Afraid she'd say no.

"You realize my helping you might cause a scandal in town. Everyone would be talking about it." She said the words without looking up.

"Yes, but I figure it's none of their business. My daughter is too important for me to care what other people think." He spoke softly, hoping she felt the same.

She faced him, her beautiful amber eyes locking with his. Everything about her tensed shoulders told him to go away. But in her eyes, he saw a blaze of empathy. And if she was the kind of woman he thought she was, she'd say yes. For Evie's sake.

"The employees down at the sawmill won't like it. Neither would my brother or mom," she said.

"I understand that, but I wouldn't ask if it weren't critically important."

In fact, he firmly believed that Evie's life and future happiness depended on this woman. Yet, he understood Jill's reticence. If personnel at the Forest Service office knew she was helping his daughter, they might talk, but they wouldn't care much. But for Jill, it was different. She'd grown up in this town. Most of her friends and family would disapprove. Even so, she didn't sound resentful, but rather mildly concerned. As though she were trying to figure out how to get around all of that nonsense. And that caused a small burgeoning of hope to rise within his chest.

"I wouldn't ask if I had any other options, Jill. I'm asking for Evie. Please. Help her."

"Can you tell me a little more about her problem?" she asked.

He shrugged. "Normally, she's fine. But that day she bolted from the convenience store, a boy wearing a black Windbreaker had come inside and she panicked."

"A black Windbreaker?"

"Yes, similar to the one the man was wearing the night he shot Lina, my wife."

Jill took a deep inhale and let it go. "I think you'd better tell me the whole story."

He hadn't expected this. He really didn't

want to talk about it. But he also knew if Jill was going to be able to help Evie, she'd have to know everything.

He braced his hands along the cushioned armrests of the chair and squeezed tight. "I was fighting wildfire deep in the wilderness of Colorado when it happened. They sent me word that Lina had been killed, then evacuated me via helicopter. It took almost two days for me to arrive home. Two long days to reach Evie. By then, she was almost catatonic. Curled in a fetal position, her unblinking eyes staring straight ahead. It took weeks for her to even acknowledge me. Once she did, we settled into a routine, but she's never spoken a word since then."

Jill winced. "And Evie watched her mother die?"

He nodded, the words shredding his heart into confetti. "She was with her mom when the convenience store was robbed. The thief was high on drugs and desperate for his next fix. He shot the sales clerk and Lina for no apparent reason. Evie hid behind the cash register counter, or he might have killed her, too."

The story rattled Brent's nerves every time he thought about it. He'd almost lost everything that day. Thankfully, he still had Evie.

"Did the police catch the guy?" Jill asked,

her lovely brows drawn together with compassion. From the stammer in her voice, Brent could tell the story upset her, too.

"Yes, the store had a camera and they caught him later that night. He's now in the state penitentiary, serving a life sentence. Unfortunately, that won't bring Lina back and Evie has never recovered."

Neither had he, for that matter. "After all this time, I still can't believe a nineteen-year-old kid murdered my wife for seventy-three dollars in the cash register and a box of chocolate-covered doughnuts."

"I'm so sorry, Brent." Jill's eyes softened, her delicate forehead crinkled.

"Yeah, thanks." He looked away, blinking his eyes fast. Wishing this woman didn't bring out these deep emotions in him. He'd never confided these things to anyone before. And he wished he could put aside what had happened in the past and move on and be happy again. But he couldn't. Not until Evie got better.

"How long has it been?" Jill asked.

"A year this month. Except for me, you're the first person Evie's shown any real emotion to since that time."

"I see." She looked away, her eyes wide and filled with sorrow.

"I've made you sad, and that wasn't my intention."

"No, it's okay," she reassured him. "I've heard a lot of sad stories with the other kids I work with. I must admit, Evie's situation is the worst. You understand I might not be able to help her."

"Yes, I understand. But I'm hoping you'll try." A spear of optimism lanced his chest. Jill hadn't said no. In fact, she sounded like she was actually contemplating saying yes.

Evie had bonded with Jill on some innate level Brent didn't understand. He felt the same, like an electric current humming between them. Perhaps it was because Jill had saved Evie. And in doing so, Jill had earned both his and Evie's trust. None of it made sense, but it did mean a lot. After all the therapy he'd dragged Evie to over the past year, she'd finally related to Jill. The person who had rescued her.

"I'm sure you've already taken her to a doctor or a psychologist, right?" Jill glanced at him but didn't quite meet his eyes.

He snorted. "Lots of them, actually. They tried their best, but I think they did Evie more harm than good. That's why I'm asking for your help."

"I don't know, Brent…"

She didn't finish, but she didn't have to. He knew what she was thinking.

"You afraid everyone in town might think we're an item? Or just that we're conspiring against them?"

Her lovely mouth twitched and, for a moment, he thought she might crack a smile. "When you put it that way, it sounds kind of ridiculous."

And irritating. He didn't want something as silly as social mores to stop her from helping Evie. "It sure does."

She laughed and he stopped breathing. Her eyes sparkled, her face radiant and beautiful. He stared at her, enthralled. Then, he found his voice. "You should do that more often."

Her smile faded.

"We could always tell them you're helping me because I'm your long-lost cousin," he said.

She lifted her brows. "My cousin?"

"Yeah, from Topeka."

She laughed again, the sound high and sweet. "You really aren't taking this very serious, are you?"

"Oh, I take it very seriously, believe me."

She wore a mock-scolding frown, but he wasn't buying it. Maybe he was reading her wrong, but he thought she wanted to help. Fear of what people might say was holding her back. A huge roadblock to what he hoped to achieve.

"I'll pay any fee you ask. Just please, try to help my daughter," he said.

She broke eye contact with him and studied a vase of daisies sitting in the middle of the coffee table. Fresh vacuum marks lined the carpet and the air smelled of furniture polish. The house looked tidy and comfy. He imagined that before Jill's father passed away, this was a happy home. Velma Crawford had told him Jill was recently divorced, and he realized she'd known a lot of sadness recently, just like him.

"Okay, I'll do it," she finally said.

He sat up straight, his senses on high alert. "You mean it? Really?"

He couldn't prevent a mixture of hope and doubt from filling his voice. He didn't dare trust his ears.

She glanced at the doorway leading to the back of the house and he got the impression she was making sure her mother wasn't standing nearby listening. Then she spoke low. "Yes, I'll do the best I can. But I can't make any promises."

He released a breathless laugh of relief. "I understand."

She stood and walked to the door, signaling

their interview was over. Taking her cue, he followed. She opened the door and stepped outside onto the front porch, speaking in a whisper. "Bring Evie to me at five-thirty each Monday, Wednesday and Friday evening. But don't bring her here to my mom's house. Take her around back to the stairs leading up to my apartment above the garage. That's where I'm staying. We can discuss some kind of fee later."

He nodded, willing to build a rocket ship and fly it to the moon if it meant Evie might get better. "You got it. We'll be here. But just one more request."

"And what's that?"

"No black Windbreakers or hoodies. When Evie sees one, she goes ballistic."

Jill nodded. "Thanks for the warning. I think we'll be okay. I don't like black hoodies either. Is Evie still using her dry-erase board?"

He lifted one shoulder. "Now and then."

"Ask her to use it whenever she wants something from you. Don't get her a glass of milk or anything else until she writes it down. I want her to get in the habit of asking you for help. That will build the necessity for her to speak. And have her bring the erase board with her for her lessons at my place."

"Okay."

She quickly gave him her cell phone number. "Call me if you need to cancel, or if Evie has a problem, or makes any kind of breakthrough, no matter how small. But don't ever call my mom's house. Agreed?"

"Agreed."

"Good. See you later."

Without another word, she turned and closed the door. Interview over with. And standing there all alone, he blinked, feeling odd and yet strangely buoyant. In spite of everything standing between them, Jill had said yes. And all of a sudden, the world was filled with magnificent possibilities.

Chapter Six

On Monday morning, Jill arrived at the Forest Service office promptly at eight o'clock. She parked her car, then went inside where Martha directed her out back into the spacious yard. She wore a jacket over her old T-shirt. The kind that didn't matter if she got it dirty or ripped. She figured planting little trees wouldn't be a clean process and she didn't want to ruin her good clothes.

Standing on the back step, she took a moment to get her bearings. She'd rarely been back here, the main artery of the Forest Service office where all the action took place.

A tall chain-link fence surrounded several Forest Service trucks, fire engines and other vehicles, all parked in straight rows. From the open garage door, she could see a workbench and a variety of tools stored in upright bins and hooks. Everything in its place. Brent certainly ran a tidy shop.

To the left, corrals butted up against a large barn and sheds, each building painted white with green trim. She rested a hand against the leather gloves tucked into the waistband of her blue jeans and breathed in the musty scent of straw and horses. A smell she found familiar and pleasing. She'd never ridden much as a child, but she'd been raised in this town and many of her friends owned farm animals.

She didn't know what to expect today. Maybe it had been a mistake to ask to help. Working all morning with people who might resent her because of her family's sawmill wouldn't be much fun. Since he was the boss, she doubted Brent would be going with the work crew up on the mountain today. That thought brought her a modicum of ease, and also disappointment.

Drafts of sunlight filtered across the lean-to by the barn. Five men ranging from young to old and wearing Forest Service uniforms, milled about the graveled yard. They laughed and talked together as they packed buckets and tools into the back of two green trucks.

Jill took a deep breath to settle her nerves. She could do this. Be pleasant, work hard and it'd be over with soon enough.

Placing her baseball cap on her head, she pulled her long ponytail through the back opening. Somehow, it helped her feel insulated from the men's curious looks. Taking a deep breath, she stepped off the back porch and went to greet them.

"Good morning," she called.

"Morning." Grant Olson waved back, a burly man Jill recognized from church. She knew he was Brent's range specialist.

"Howdy." A couple of other men nodded with tentative smiles.

Deep laughter came from the corrals. She turned, catching sight of Brent and a young man of perhaps nineteen years of age standing near a dun-colored horse. As usual, Brent wore his ranger's uniform. The brass shield pinned to his chest gleamed in the bright sunlight. A reminder of who he was and the difficulties he could press upon her family if he chose. Thank goodness he didn't seem to be a vindictive man.

She studied his strong profile. The intensity of his locked jaw and tall, athletic body. Without intending to, she had to do a double take.

"I was surprised to hear you were gonna help us today," Grant said.

He didn't need to explain why. Jill understood. But she shrugged, brushing it off. "I just want to help."

He grunted. "Well, that's a first. Usually you loggers avoid us like the plague."

A dozen snippy retorts came to mind, but she bit her tongue instead. She didn't want any more contention in her life. But she still felt as though she didn't belong here.

Her gaze strayed to the corrals again. While the teenager fetched a can of oats, Brent wielded a pitchfork. He broke off two flakes from a bale of hay before spearing it into the feeding trough. His long-sleeved shirt tightened across his muscular back. It was several seconds before Jill realized she was staring. She scuffed a booted foot against the dirt, feeling nervous. She considered going inside and telling Martha she had to cancel today.

The horse lifted its head from the trough, chewing a mouthful of hay in serene detachment. Brent reached up and rubbed the animal's soft muzzle. He spoke low, and she wondered what he was saying to the horse. And she figured a man that was kind to animals couldn't be all that bad, even if he was the forest ranger.

"What can I do?" she asked Grant.

"You can load those into the truck." Grant pointed at several shovels lying on the ground.

At the sound of their voices, Brent turned. She didn't acknowledge him, but felt his gaze resting on her like a leaden weight. She ignored him and picked up the hand tools. Out of her peripheral vision, she watched him open the corral gate, then latch it securely behind him. She laid the shovels in the truck bed, conscious of him walking toward her with that forest ranger swagger of confidence. Prickles of sensation rushed from the back of her neck and down her spine.

"Hi, Jill. Glad you could join us today." His deep voice sounded cheerful, and she suspected it had something to do with her agreeing to work with Evie later that evening.

"Hello," she returned.

She couldn't deny a desire to give back to nature after taking so much. Her family's mill harvested thousands of trees. Their contracts demanded they pay for contractors to plant new seedlings. It was a state law, after all. For every tree cut down, a new seedling must be planted in its place.

Unless the trees were stolen. No one paid for that except the taxpayers. And Jill hated the devastation she'd seen up on Cove Mountain that day she'd given Evie the dry-erase board. It wouldn't hurt Jill to help replant. And her efforts might go a long way toward soothing angry feelings with the Forest Service.

Jill tugged on her gloves and reached for a bucket filled with little ponderosa pine seedlings. She struggled to lift the heavy weight over to the truck. Muddy water sloshed over the edge. Brent took hold of the handle and lifted it for her.

"You'll hurt your back lifting heavy objects like that," he advised.

She stood back and bristled, trying not to take offense. After all, the bucket had been hefty. "If you do my work for me, I won't be much help today."

"Don't worry. There'll be plenty for you to do up on the mountain."

His lips twitched, and something warm and mushy softened inside her chest. He was just trying to be helpful, and she decided not to take offense. "You're going with us, too?"

He must have sensed her reticence, because he showed a doubtful frown. "Today I am. The crew's almost finished with the planting and I need to check on their progress. Is that okay with you?"

"Yes, of course. You're the boss and can do whatever you want." She spoke quickly, feeling rather foolish. Her pulse raced through her veins and her stomach swirled. She couldn't ignore this man, yet she couldn't quite let down her guard with him either.

Disregarding the chaos in her mind, she set to work, helping lift a large cooler of bottled water into the truck. Once they had everything loaded, Jill sat in the backseat, sandwiched between two young college students who were new summer employees. With five people along, conversation was easy. Jill didn't have to speak. She listened as the men discussed the Boise Hawks. The professional baseball team had taken the division title the year before. An avid fan, Brent hoped they could do it again. Hearing him talk about baseball made him seem so normal and masculine.

"What about you, Jill? Do you like the Hawks?" Sitting in the driver's seat, he looked in the rearview mirror at her.

"Yeah, sure I do. Who doesn't like the Hawks?" Actually, she rarely missed a game. Just one more thing they had in common.

Within an hour, they passed the cutblock where Jill's mill was cutting timber. Seeing the large logging trucks and heavy equipment moving across the landing zone gave her a modicum of peace. If Brent thought Alan was guilty of theft, he would have shut them down first thing. Which would stop mill production and lead to bankruptcy.

Another fifteen minutes, and they arrived at the site of desolation. Jill was pleasantly surprised to see that the work crew had already planted a considerable area of seedlings in the past few days since she was up here last.

Brent killed the engine and threw the door open wide. He got out and reached a hand to help Jill climb down. She hesitated, but then accepted his offer. During the drive here, she'd removed her gloves. She regretted that now as the feel of his warm fingers twined around hers. A strange, giddy sensation filled her chest.

"Thank you." She pulled away the moment she was standing in the dirt.

"Have you ever planted seedlings before?" While they unloaded the equipment, Brent explained their work.

"No, I'm afraid not," she said.

He reached up and lifted two buckets of seedlings out of the truck. "That's okay. It's not a complicated process. You'll pick it up fast. Until you get the hang of it, we can work as a team. One person digs the hole, the other person plants the seedling. You'll be my partner today."

"Okay." What else could she say? He was in charge and seemed so confident.

To keep from staring at his handsome face,

she copied the other men and busied herself by tugging tools out of the truck and laying them in a neat pile at the side of the road.

"This is a dibble bar. It's what we use to dig the holes for planting bare-root tree seedlings." Brent held up a strange-looking hand tool that incorporated a T-handle at the top of the bar and a straight, flat edge at the bottom.

Taking a bucket of seedlings with him, Brent walked over to the nearest row where the men resumed their planting. They spaced the seed-lings apart every eight to ten feet.

"A picture is worth a thousand words. Watch what I do, and then I'll explain a few things to you," he said.

She obediently watched while he thrust the straight edge of the dibble bar straight down to slice it into the damp earth. He then pushed the handle forward, to create a V-shape in the dirt.

He nodded at the bucket. "Can you grab one of those seedlings for me?"

She did so, ignoring the drip of murky water on her bare hands. A happy feeling thrummed through her as she got her fingers dirty. It felt good to be working with nature. She'd been cooped up inside her house and a stuffy office in Boise for too long. She needed this time off. To feel good again. To breathe in great drafts of cool mountain air.

"We don't want to plant a sick tree. It won't thrive. But this seedling is healthy. Notice the green color and soft bristles of the little branches?" He pointed as he spoke and she nodded.

Using a sharp pocket knife, he pruned off an inch of growth at the bottom of the roots.

"If the roots are longer than the hole, we'll end up with J-rooting, and the tree won't grow well. The roots must go straight down into the ground, with no curve at the bottom." He nodded at the hole and handed the seedling back to her, his hand brushing against hers.

While he held the dibble bar, she placed the seedling into the hole.

"Pull it up just a bit so the top of the hole is even with the root collar of the seedling," he instructed.

She tugged the miniature tree up a half inch. He brushed against her shoulder as he moved the dibble bar toward himself and then back toward the seedling, pulling dirt in around the roots. Then, he used the heel of his heavy boot to tamp dirt in, nice and firm.

"That will pack soil tight around the roots and get rid of any air pockets," he said.

"Do we need to water the little tree?"

He shook his head. "Nope, the ground is damp enough. It'll be fine."

She stared transfixed at the seedling planted happily in the ground. "That's sure an easy process."

"It is. Not much to it. You want to do another?" He grinned and she thought he enjoyed this project as much as she did.

They worked for some time in companionable silence. Now and then, Brent advised her if something wasn't quite right. He reached around her, resting one hand lightly against the middle of her back. So gentle that it might have been a caress.

Looking up, she caught Grant watching them, a slight smile playing at the corners of his brusque mouth. Heat flooded her cheeks and she stepped away.

"That seedling doesn't have a clean, earthy smell. It stinks, which means its roots are probably rotting. And notice its little branches are starting to yellow?" Brent brushed his fingers across the bristles, which fell off and dusted the ground. He didn't seem to notice the other men watching them.

She crouched down on her haunches and quirked her brows up at him. "You think it's dying?"

"I do." He handed her a healthy one.

She slid the roots into the ground, he tamped the dirt around the plant, and off they went.

Time passed quickly, the buoyant voices of the other men filtering around her as they worked. By the time they'd planted all the seedlings they'd brought, Jill felt surprisingly light and carefree.

"You thirsty?" Brent offered her a bottle of water.

"Yes, thank you." She popped the lid and gulped down half the liquid before taking a deep breath.

"Can you believe it'll take eighty years for these trees to mature?" He spoke between swallows as they stood side by side and inspected the area they'd planted.

"Yes, it's amazing," she agreed, lifting her cap and wiping her forehead. "One day, when I'm a very old woman, I want to come up here and view all the trees I helped plant today."

He smiled, looking askance at her. Without warning, he reached out and brushed aside a stray curl that had escaped her long ponytail. Then, he gave a quick tug on the brim of her baseball cap. An affectionate gesture that left her feeling suddenly shy.

"Me, too. I love my work as a ranger. There's no profession like it in the world. These ponderosa pines will put down deep roots. Some will grow to ninety feet tall before another ranger lets a sawmill come in and cut them down. And then the process will be repeated. That's how we manage our renewable resources."

For a brief moment, his words saddened her. The thought of their hard work being cut down seemed counterproductive. Then, she reminded herself that these trees would one day provide a warm house for someone to live in. Or an office building. A fence post, a broomstick or a desk. And each of those items provided jobs for people. Livelihoods for entire families and a healthy economy. Those things were important, too. And as long as they replanted, the tree population would continue to thrive. Without Brent to oversee these natural resources, they would be abused and the ecology in the area would fall out of balance.

She contemplated how fragile life was and how much she had to thank God for. The past year had been difficult, no doubt about it. Her divorce and losing her dad had made her rather cynical. She'd all but abandoned her beliefs in the Lord. But being out here with Brent helped renew her faith.

"I'm glad you're ensuring we replenish what we take away."

He smiled at that. "Many people don't see it that way. They think I'm here to prevent them from using our natural resources. But

I'm not a preservationist. I'm a conservation-ist. I believe in using our resources, but managing them so we don't destroy everything for future generations."

His declaration surprised her. "Do you mean that?"

"Absolutely. It's how I've always done my business as a ranger. I want to let your mill harvest trees, but not to the point of abuse. That's why I'm here. To keep it all in balance."

She nodded. "I wholeheartedly agree with that philosophy."

"Good. I'm glad we can agree on that." Again, he flashed that devastating smile that made her heart pump furiously.

She contemplated the pillaged forest with its fresh planting of seedlings and what the baby trees might become within a couple of decades. They'd grow and thicken. Deer, elk and birds would return. Shade from the trees would create healthy spawning beds for fish in the streams and rivers. And in that moment, she realized she and Brent weren't worlds apart after all. Not if they could agree on something as important as this.

No matter what else happened, working with Brent today had taught Jill a lesson. First, they had a lot in common. And second, the more time she spent with this charming forest ranger, the more she liked him.

That afternoon, Brent picked Evie up at Mrs. Crawford's place promptly at five-fifteen. He didn't want to be late for Evie's first appointment with Jill. Ten minutes later, he parked a half block down from Jill's mother's house and walked with Evie to the backyard. They easily found the stairs leading to the upper level of the detached garage, where Jill said she was staying.

"You think you'll like visiting with Jill for a while?" he asked Evie as he took her hand.

The girl's ponytail bounced as she nodded, a smile curling the corners of her mouth. She carried her little dry-erase board under her arm, though she didn't use it to communicate with anyone but him. He'd rather hoped she might draw pictures and use it to talk with Mrs. Crawford, but she'd refused. And he sensed it had something to do with trust.

"I'm glad." He squeezed her hand as they climbed the stairs. He hoped this was good for her and silently prayed she responded positively to Jill's teaching.

At this point, he didn't know what to expect. When he'd asked Jill to help Evie, he'd expected her to say no. He still couldn't believe she'd agreed and realized it was a gigantic imposition on her. But he wondered if she'd told her mother that she'd be working with Evie.

At the top of the stairs, he stood on the landing with Evie and knocked. Over time, he'd learned to read his daughter's silent language. She stared at the door, her body vibrating with nervous energy. He rested one hand against her shoulder, to offer reassurance. He didn't know how she might react and was prepared to stay with her, if necessary.

The door opened and Jill stood there wearing a clean shirt, blue jeans and white tennis shoes. After spending the morning up on the mountain planting seedlings, she'd gotten dirty, but had obviously cleaned up. Her sandy-blond hair was lying about her shoulders in silky curling waves he longed to thread his fingers through.

"Evie!" Jill flashed a happy smile and went down on one knee to greet his daughter.

Evie launched herself into Jill's arms, hugging her neck tight. Brent breathed a sigh of relief. He'd been worried Jill or Evie might change their minds and back out on these lessons. If that happened, he didn't know what he'd do.

"I've got some fun activities planned for you.

You want to stay and play with me for a while?" Jill asked, looking deep into Evie's eyes.

The girl nodded. Brent liked how Jill made this a game rather than a stoic office visit. No wonder Evie responded so well. And yet, he knew his child's relationship with Jill was so much more.

"Ah-ah, use the dry-erase board to tell me what you want. Do you want to stay and play with me for a while?" Jill pointed at the board Evie still clutched under her arm.

Evie obediently wrote the word *yes* on the board.

"Good. Then, come on inside." Jill stood and stepped aside.

Evie hesitated and Brent feared she might refuse. That notion quickly flew right out the window as Evie walked into the apartment without a backward glance. He watched from the doorway as she pulled out a chair and sat up to a small wooden table laden with an assortment of papers, crayons, markers and books. She set her dry-erase board aside but didn't touch the other art supplies.

"Hi, there." Jill flashed him a smile.

"Hi." He glanced over her shoulder at the tidy, one-room apartment with a table, sofa and chairs. He figured the couch must be a fold-out she slept on. No kitchen or bathroom, from what he could tell. But he distinctly caught the tantalizing fragrance of her delicate perfume and he took a deep inhale.

"Looks like Evie is making herself right at home," she said.

"Yeah, I'm so glad."

"Have you been insisting that Evie use her dry-erase board when she wants something?" Jill spoke low, for Brent's ears alone.

"Yes, I have."

"Good. I'm hoping that will lead to her finally using her voice. Ideally, it'd be best if Mrs. Crawford could do the same thing. Evie might refuse at first, but I think if we're persistent, she'll start asking for specific things instead of nodding *yes* or *no*."

He hoped so. "We'll keep using it. What time should I pick her up?"

"Give us one hour," Jill said.

"Sounds good. Evie? I'm going now, sweetheart." He called in a louder voice, to get the girl's attention. He wanted to make sure she knew he was leaving. He didn't want to merely disappear and have the girl fall into a screaming fit. That wouldn't be fair to Jill, even if she was trained to deal with such situations.

Evie glanced up and waved goodbye, like this was an everyday occurrence. No big deal. Brent stared, unable to believe how at ease she seemed, in spite of this new environment. He released a sigh of relief. For now, Evie was okay. He just hoped she stayed that way.

He turned and left, conscious of Jill closing the door behind him. Fearing Evie might change her mind and fall apart, he sat and dozed in his truck, staying nearby in case the worst happened. Exactly one hour later, he returned.

As he rounded the corner of the garage, he looked up and could see the door to Jill's apartment stood wide open. Angry voices came from inside. He gripped the handrail of the stairs and paused on the bottom step.

"I can't believe you agreed to tutor the forest ranger's daughter. What were you thinking?"

Brent recognized Arline Russell's voice. Obviously Jill's mother was inside her apartment, and she wasn't happy.

"I was thinking about Evie. She needs help, Mom. My help. Besides, it's the Christian thing to do," Jill responded.

"But she's the ranger's brat."

Brent flinched. Hearing his precious daughter called a brat twisted inside his gut.

"He wants to throw your brother in jail. Is that what you want?" Arline's voice trembled, as though she were near tears.

"Of course not. I don't believe that, Mom.

He hasn't even charged Alan with anything yet," Jill soothed.

"He will. Mark my words. If he can, he'll do it."

"No, Mom. Brent isn't like that. I've been around him enough to know he's a kind man. He's not out to hurt us. He's just doing his job the best way he knows how. But we've got to meet him halfway."

Brent's fingers tightened around the handrail. Jill's words touched him deeply. He appreciated her trust and vote of confidence, but there was no way on earth he was going to stand by and let Arline bash him in front of his child.

Bounding up the stairs two at a time, he stood in the doorway and clenched his hands. He gritted his teeth, trying to retain his temper.

"Brent!" Jill glanced over her mother's shoulder.

"I'm here to pick up Evie." He spoke low, his gaze resting on Arline. With narrowed eyes, he dared her to say one more derogatory thing about him. He didn't want to lose Jill as a friend, but he wouldn't tolerate this situation any longer.

Arline's face drained of color. Without another word, she huffed and brushed past him, tromping down the steps and scurrying toward the back door of her house.

"Where's my daughter?" He glanced around the apartment, searching for Evie. She wasn't here and he didn't know if he should be alarmed or relieved.

"Evie's fine. She's in Mom's house, using the restroom," Jill said.

He arched a brow. "Alone? By herself?"

"Yes. I took her in, but she told me she could stay by herself. She knows the way."

He tilted his head in amazement. "She said that?"

Jill pointed at the table. "On her dry-erase board. I'm sorry you heard all of that. But don't worry. Mom won't say anything cruel to Evie. She'd never pick on an innocent child."

He had his doubts. But right now, he was still in shock. He couldn't believe Evie had stayed in the house by herself. Strange environments usually upset her. She always clung to him, refusing to leave his side. But now, he didn't want her alone with Arline Russell.

"I need to go get her." He pivoted on his heels.

Jill touched his arm, a soothing gesture that seemed to burn through his skin. "It's okay. I took her into the house and gave her a tour. Mom gave her milk and chocolate chip cookies and read her a story. I hope that's okay. In spite of what you might think, they've become friends."

His frown deepened. "Your mother read Evie a story?"

Jill nodded. "Yes, I was there. It's part of the protocol I'm working on, to show Evie that she can trust other people. Mom's a very nice woman, most of the time. She's a natural with Evie."

He jabbed his fingers through his hair, feeling confused. Right now, he didn't know what to believe. Arline hated him, but read stories to Evie. And the fact that his daughter had stayed here and gone to use the bathroom by herself was a giant indicator that she felt safe. She was gaining more confidence. A distinct improvement. But even if she wasn't aware of Arline's dislike for him, he wasn't about to leave his child where she wasn't wanted.

"I don't want her to accidentally overhear your mother speaking about me like that," he said.

"She won't," Jill reassured him. "Actually, this was my fault. I didn't give Mom much warning. She knew I was working with a child that had experienced trauma in her life, but she didn't know Evie belonged to you."

So, because Evie was his daughter, Arline

didn't want the girl here. And yet she recognized Evie was innocent in this matter. But the woman's hatred for him was enough incentive for Brent to whisk Evie away and never return.

"I think this was a huge mistake." He turned to go collect Evie and take her home.

"Please wait!" Jill tugged more aggressively on his arm, pulling him back.

He wanted to resist. To yell and scream at her. He'd trusted her with his child, and look what had happened. She'd defended him to her mother, but he feared what might happen if Evie were to eavesdrop and overhear bad things. He shuddered to contemplate how it might set her back.

"I'll talk with Mom. This won't happen again," Jill promised.

He relaxed a bit, telling himself it wasn't Jill's fault Arline didn't like him. Jill had been nothing but kind to Evie. But he couldn't afford to take any more chances. No, not ever again.

"Look!" Jill held up a piece of paper covered with black, ugly scribbles.

He stared at the angry, dark lines. Then, he reached out and took the page, his hand trembling. "Did...did Evie draw this?"

She nodded. "It's very telling, don't you think?"

Yes, it was so hideous that he wanted to

weep at the sadness of it all. And yet, he also knew this was significant.

"Does she color like this at home?" Jill asked.

He shook his head. "No, she never colors. At home or at school. That's why I was so surprised when she accepted the dry-erase board and actually wrote on it for you."

Jill released a pensive sigh. "Just as I thought. I think today was a great success. We've made a lot of progress, Brent."

"We have?" He couldn't see how. Not fully.

"Yes, this picture is a reflection of the feelings Evie is keeping bottled up inside herself. Today, she released a lot of that by drawing this design. She let Mom hold her on her lap while they read a story together. And when I asked, she said she wanted to go potty by herself. For a normal kid, that isn't a big deal. But all of that for Evie is a major advancement."

He stared at the hideous artwork, if you could call it art. For a normal child, it was worthy of the trash bin. But it was the first drawing Evie had made since before her mother died. And then, he realized what Jill said was true. A significance he would have missed entirely, without her expert analysis. He was amazed at Jill's insight. Amazed that she'd succeeded where he'd failed so many times.

"Don't take her away from me, Brent. Not yet. I really think if you'll let me work with her some more, I can help her. I just need more time."

"But what about your mom?" He lifted a hand toward the door, feeling helpless and hopeful at the same time. He wanted to trust Jill. He really did. But what if she was wrong? What if Evie got worse? He didn't know what he'd do then.

"I can handle Mom. She's frightened and hurt. She feels threatened by you and is only trying to protect Alan, the same way you're trying to protect Evie. But she's a kind woman and she loves children."

"She called Evie a brat."

"She didn't mean it, Brent. She was just upset. I'm asking you to trust me."

Trust. Something neither he nor Evie had done in a very long time.

"If you continue working with Evie, it might get rougher on you," he said. "People in town are bound to find out you're helping me. Many of them won't like it."

Lifting her chin, Jill folded her arms. Her amber eyes flashed with stubborn persistence. "Don't worry. I can handle them. You leave it to me."

Footsteps sounded on the stairs outside.

Anxious to see his daughter, Brent stepped out on the landing with Jill close behind. Arline stood at the bottom of the steps, watching closely as Evie climbed up and threw her arms around her father's waist.

Hugging Evie tight, Brent gazed down at Arline. For a moment, he saw compassion crinkling the woman's eyes. Then, she glanced at him and the kindness faded. She didn't huff this time, but turned around and stomped off, her shoulders slumped in defeat. Brent realized she'd been watching over his daughter. Making sure she was safe while she navigated the steep stairs. Which seemed odd after the bad things she'd said about him. Maybe Jill was right. Maybe Arline's anger wasn't directed at Evie.

"Did you have fun with Jill?" Brent drew back and gazed into his daughter's eyes, searching for the truth there.

Evie smiled and nodded. Calm as a summer's morning. Not a hint of anger, fear or worry.

"Did you read a story with Mrs. Russell?" he asked.

Another nod, and then Evie laughed, the sound low and sweet. He stared at her, shocked and delighted. Feeling so emotional that he actually felt the burn of tears. Her laughter was still new to him. He hugged her again, holding her close for several long, wonderful seconds. He longed to ask what the story was about. Obviously it had amused her. But that could wait until they were home.

Taking the girl's hand, he faced Jill. She stood apart, shifting her weight, her arms folded, her face drawn with apprehension. Anxious with fear that he might take Evie away and never return.

And then something occurred to him. Out of all the doctors and specialists he'd dragged Evie to, she'd screamed and cried with everyone. And when he'd returned to take her away from their sessions, he'd seen the relief in their eyes. They'd been glad to get rid of Evie. She was a problem child they had difficulty coping with. A nuisance they didn't want. Instead of breaking through the steel wall Evie had built around herself, they'd prescribed drugs to sedate her. To make her malleable and quiet. Several had even suggested he lock Evie in an asylum for troubled kids. Of course, Brent had refused. He would never give up on her. Not ever. And then, when she went to Mrs. Crawford's house without a problem, he started to think Evie might have a future. That she could get better.

Not one specialist had done Evie a lick of good. Jill was the first person that seemed genuinely concerned and desperate to help. Even if Arline hated him, he couldn't deny that Jill made a difference. And he wouldn't take that away from Evie. Not now. Not when they were so close to making even more breakthroughs.

"Thank you for all that you've done," he said to Jill.

She blinked her gentle brown eyes, her forehead creased with worry. "You're welcome."

"Evie, tell Jill thank you," he instructed.

The girl hugged Jill, but didn't say a word. Then she took Brent's hand, ready to leave.

"If it's okay, I'll bring her over again on Wednesday evening," he said.

Jill's face softened. When she spoke, her voice sounded breathless with relief. "That will be fine."

Another laugh came from Evie and he whirled around to stare at the girl in amazement. Jill laughed, too, the sound infectious. For several moments, they stood there and laughed at nothing. Just enjoying the sound of their voices.

Jill gave one nod, a soft smile curving her lips. But in her eyes, he saw her understanding. She knew what this meant to him and Evie.

"Thanks again." He led Evie down the stairs.

In his heart, he knew it was the right thing to bring Evie back. But a prickle of fear still nipped at his mind. At the bottom of the stairs, he looked over his shoulder. Jill stood on the top landing, watching them go. She lifted a hand and waved. Evie didn't see it, but Brent did. And he couldn't help thinking Jill was the most amazing woman he'd ever met.

Yes, Evie's drawing was nothing but angry, dark scrawls. But at least she'd told Jill what she was feeling inside. And she'd laughed not once, but twice. Jill had achieved what no one else had done, including himself and Mrs. Crawford. She'd pulled Evie out of her hard shell and gotten her to finally communicate.

Chapter Seven

"Good morning, Mom." Jill stepped inside the back door of the kitchen to her mother's house. Arline sat at the table wearing her lavender bathrobe and blue fuzzy slippers. Her dark-blond hair lay in damp tendrils around her shoulders. No doubt she'd already showered and was letting it air dry.

Looking up from the morning paper, Arline didn't smile as she indicated a pitcher of orange juice sitting on the table. "Fresh squeezed. Help yourself."

Jill retrieved a glass from the cupboard and came to sit across from her mother. Mom laid the paper on the table, watching as Jill poured half a glass of juice. She took several swallows before lowering the glass and holding it with both hands.

"Mom, we need to talk."

Arline met her daughter's eyes. "Yes, we do. After everything we've been through, why would you help that man? Your father would turn over in his grave if he knew."

Jill blinked, surprised by her mother's directness. But that was one of the things she loved most about her mom. Arline never pretended and always told the truth. But she also frequently said things that shouldn't be said, because they hurt too much and weren't constructive.

"I'm helping Evie, his daughter." Jill quickly explained about Evie's mother being killed in an armed robbery a year earlier and the trauma it had caused both the ranger and his little girl.

"That's very sad. I can't imagine how horrible that must be for Evie and...and the ranger," Mom said.

Wow! That was a huge concession for her mother to make.

"So you can see why I agreed to help. Honestly, I didn't think it mattered who Evie's father is. She needs help and that's all that's important right now," Jill said.

"But she's the forest ranger's daughter, Jill. If she's here, he'll be here, too."

"I understand, but I can't hold that against the little girl. I help children. It's what I'm trained to do, Mom. You know that."

Jill braced herself for a storm, expecting tears and yelling and harsh words. But Mom surprised her when she sat back and pressed her fingers against her mouth, quietly thinking this through.

"Is Evie getting any better?" Arline asked.

Jill nodded. "Yes, I've seen some amazing progress just since I met her. I don't know why, but yesterday, she responded well to every activity I gave her. And she adores you. Brent said it was amazing that Evie let you hold her while you read her a story."

A bit of flattery might help, but Jill wouldn't say it if it wasn't true. Evie liked Mom, that was apparent. She felt safe here. In time, Jill hoped Evie learned to trust most people again. At least enough to start speaking and have a normal, happy life.

Mom blinked and looked down, the corners of her mouth turning up in a slight smile. "I'm not surprised she's responded well to you, Jill. You always were good with kids. I always thought you'd get married and have a passel of them. Then you got divorced instead."

"Mom, David didn't want kids. You know that. And I couldn't stay with someone that didn't love me. He was cheating on me."

Arline's jaw hardened. "No, he never was good enough for you. I'm glad he's gone. And

I'm so glad your college education has paid off. It was the right thing to get you out of this town so you could have a future. I think Evie's lucky to have my precious daughter to help her out."

Hearing such words of praise from her mother caused a liquid warmth to suffuse Jill's chest. When she'd first left for college, Mom had fought it and asked her not to go. To stay here in town and work at the mill. But Jill had hungered for an education. She wanted a different life. To see and do new things and meet a man that wasn't from a small, backward town like Bartlett. David had been in law school when they met. He'd swept her off her feet and taken her to Europe for their honeymoon. Since the divorce, she had a different perspective—on almost everything.

Maybe living in Bartlett wasn't so bad after all.

"Do you mean that, Mom?" She quirked one brow and studied her mother's serene face.

Arline nodded. "Yes, I do. I love you, Jill. And I trust you. I miss your dad more than I can say. And I may be worried about your brother and the mill, but I'm not an ogre. If your work might help Evie get better, then you should continue. And if anyone complains about it, they can come and talk to me. I'll set them straight."

Jill stared at her mother's face in astonishment, stunned by the woman's support. "Thank you, Mom."

Arline gave a calming sigh. "You're welcome. Children take precedence over pride. And Evie's been through enough. I know you can help her. But her father's a different matter."

Oh, boy. Here it comes, Jill thought.

"I don't want that man inside my house. Evie's welcome here anytime. She's too young to know any better. But you keep the forest ranger outside. At least until this theft issue is resolved."

Okay, Arline had laid down the law. But Jill didn't think her demands were so outrageous.

"Agreed. But I have my own condition. You mustn't bad-mouth Brent anymore. I don't want to take the risk that Evie might overhear."

"All right, I've told you what I think and won't say any more," Arline agreed.

Jill glanced at the rooster clock hanging on the wall over the stove and gasped. "Is that the time? I better get over to the mill."

Jill stood and gave her mother a big hug, kissing her on the cheek. Mom's slightly damp hair smelled of the coconut shampoo she'd used. Her mother's support and confidence meant so much. It meant everything. But Jill wouldn't press the issue. At least not until Alan was cleared of timber theft. She could work with Evie, but Brent would need to stick to her apartment above the garage.

Two hours later, the drone of the laser printer filled Jill's ears. Sitting at the back desk in the office at the sawmill, she cross-checked the payroll to balance the books. They had just enough money to pay their bills. So far, so good.

"Um, Jill?"

She glanced up and smiled at Ida, who stood in front of her desk. "I think we're gonna make it this month."

Ida nodded, but she didn't smile. In fact, her gray eyes crinkled with worry, her face pale. She jutted her chin toward the front door. "We've got visitors."

Jill jerked her head toward the reception counter and peered beyond Ida's shoulder. Brent stood there watching her. He was accompanied by another man wearing a similar uniform, except that he had a gold shield pinned above the flap of his left-front shirt pocket. Without thinking, Jill's gaze automatically lowered to the stranger's waist. He wore an official black radio and baton on his left hip, and a gun holstered on his right. Jill immediately recognized him for what he was. A Forest Service law enforcement officer. LEO for short. She didn't know his name, but she knew his purpose. He was here to investigate the timber theft.

To investigate Alan.

Jill popped out of her chair, a blaze of panic rushing through her veins. Brent had told her a LEO was coming in this week to explore the theft issue. Even with that warning, she still felt blindsided to have them appear out of the blue like this.

Trying to appear casual, she walked to the front of the room, her gaze clashing, then locking with Brent's. She caught no censure there, but a bland, stoic expression that neither accused, nor apologized for this intrusion. He was the forest ranger, after all. He had a job to do. But she didn't have to like it.

Dressed in his ranger's uniform with the bronze shield, Brent looked imposing and official. Nothing at all like the gentle, worried father she'd seen at her house last night.

"Hi, Jill. I'd like to introduce you to John McLaughlin. He's with the Forest Service LEI." Brent spoke in a congenial voice as he jerked his thumb toward the law officer.

A tall man with an angular jaw and piercing brown eyes, John reached out. She shook his hand and pasted a stiff smile on her face.

"Hello." The glint of John's law enforcement shield caught her eye and she blinked. She refused to look down at his gun, forcing herself to instead meet his eyes.

The man didn't smile, but he spoke pleasantly enough. "I'm sorry for the imposition, but I'd like to take a look around."

It wasn't a request. Jill knew she could refuse him, but then he'd get a court order. This situation could turn ugly if she didn't cooperate.

"Sure, I think we can accommodate you." She tensed, wishing Alan wasn't working up on the mountain today. She'd been living in Boise for so many years, she wasn't sure where to start. The office had always been her domain. Dad and Alan always dealt with the mill.

She turned and glanced into Frank Casewell's office. He was the mill manager. With his back to the door, Frank held the phone receiver to his ear and reclined in his chair, his booted feet up on his desk. No wonder the old wood was covered with deep gouges. She didn't like the way this man treated their furniture and planned to say so once they were alone. She hadn't been here when Alan had hired Frank right after Dad's death. Alan had assured her the man was experienced and came highly recommended, but she had her doubts. From what she'd witnessed during the few days she'd been back in the office, she figured Frank's work ethic left a lot to be desired.

"Frank," she called to him, knowing he might ignore her otherwise.

His feet thudded to the floor. Without turning to acknowledge her, he gave an annoyed wave of his grimy hand. "In a minute."

Jill gritted her teeth, feeling irritated. She didn't like the way this man diminished her by ignoring her authority. As a half owner of the mill, she had the power to fire him. But he didn't seem to care.

Swiveling on her heels, she faced Brent and the LEO, trying to smile. Trying to appear agreeable and helpful. "Frank's our mill manager. He'll be with us directly."

Brent's eyes narrowed and she got the impression he didn't like the way Frank treated her either. Ordinarily, Jill wouldn't have noticed. But she'd been around Brent enough times that she was learning to read his moods.

"It might be easier if you just tell me what you're looking for," she said.

John slid his left hand into his pants pocket, his intelligent gaze resting on her like a loaded cannon. "Right now, I'm not looking for anything in particular. I'd like to see your operations, nothing more. I just want to take a look around."

Was that supposed to make her feel better? He provided no useful information. She got the impression he was playing it cool. Waiting to see if she would cooperate or if it appeared the mill was hiding something.

Frank hung up the phone and he sauntered out into the main office. A short man, with a heavy black beard and long, shaggy hair. Logging was a grubby profession, but Frank's blue jeans and shirt were splotched by grease, sawdust and ketchup. He looked like he hadn't changed his wardrobe in days.

"What's up?" He shoved his grungy hands into his pants pockets. A sullen expression pulled his bushy eyebrows down into a deep V-shape. He glanced around the room in shifty squints but never quite met anyone's eyes directly.

Jill made the introductions. "Frank can take you on a tour of the mill."

Frank scratched his beard. "No can do. We got a band saw out of alignment right now. I got to go work on that first."

She gaped at him, feeling confused and flustered. If a saw was giving them problems, why hadn't he already headed out to work on it pronto? With a saw out of commission, production came to a standstill. Which meant employees were standing around shooting the breeze on the company's dime.

"Why didn't you tell me about this earlier?" she asked.

He shrugged. "I told Alan."

"Alan left to go up on the mountain over two hours ago. Why aren't you out solving the problem?"

She didn't want to have this conversation in front of Brent and John, but the words slipped out of her mouth before she could stop them.

He glared at her like she was something slimy on the bottom of his boot. "I've been on the phone, ordering a new part."

For two hours? She couldn't believe what she was hearing, but bit her tongue. It wouldn't look good to deal with the issue now.

She glanced at Brent, conscious of Ida and Karen sitting at their desks, ducking their heads to pretend they weren't listing to every single word. For the umpteenth time that day, Jill wondered why her brother had hired Frank. She'd tried to stick to the office and let Alan run the mill, but that might need to change. The minute Alan returned, she'd have a long talk with him about this problem.

She released a short sigh. "Okay, I'll take them on a tour, but go out and repair the saw right now."

Wanting to make her point, she sounded professional but demanding. Asking please wouldn't work in this case. Not when Frank wasn't doing his job. Not if they lost a day of production.

Frank shrugged and reached for the doorknob, seeming unconcerned. "Yeah, sure. See you later."

He left, and Jill took a deep breath to settle her nerves. Turning toward the coat rack, she grabbed three yellow hard hats. She placed one on her head, then handed the other two to Brent and John.

"No one out in the yard without a hard hat. OSHA regulations." Brent and John should be experienced at this job and know the drill. She was relieved when they placed their hats on their heads without comment.

This situation was new to Jill. She'd never conducted a tour of the mill for a law enforcement officer. And she'd never missed her father more than she did in that moment.

Conscious of Brent's gaze following her, she issued a few quick instructions to Ida. "I've just printed the last batch of checks. If you wouldn't mind going through them to make sure there are no mistakes, I'd appreciate it. And radio Frank in an hour to see if the saw's been fixed. Give me a call to let me know its status."

"You bet I will." Ida nodded, her stern expression indicating she understood the problem only too well and didn't like it either.

Jill hated checking up on Frank and having Ida tattle on the man, but their precarious financial position was too important to ignore.

"Shall we go?" Jill faced the two forestry men.

Brent opened the door and stood back. "Ladies first."

She caught the smile in his tone, but still felt as though she were walking out to the executioner's block. She only hoped that the LEO found everything in order. Right now, she didn't know what to expect.

The first place they went was to look at the log decks. The enormous claws of the heavy-lift logstacker unloaded trees from a truck that had come in an hour earlier. Smaller forklifts picked up logs and jetted them over to the barkers and trim saws, to remove the bark and cut the logs.

John snapped a series of pictures. As a certified cruiser, he measured the volume of various tree trunks. Jill knew if he found anything out of order, he'd be the one to testify against them in a court of law.

"How often do you have trucks coming in?" he asked.

"Right now, we're averaging five or six loads per day. But that should more than double now that summer is here and the mud is clearing off the mountains."

He inclined his head and rested his palm against the rough bark of a ponderosa pine. They called it a pumpkin, an enormous, valuable tree with few flaws in the trunk. He scraped his fingernail against a round splotch of paint at the base of the saw cut. It was the mark put there by the Forest Service to say it was okay to harvest this tree. When he reached inside his pants pocket and pulled out a small dropper vial, Jill widened her eyes in fascinated horror.

Oh, no. He was going to check the tracer paint.

Tracer paint was used to indicate boundary lines and which trees were approved by the Forest Service to be harvested. Embedded with a special element, the paint was proof that this tree was cut legally. But thieves often falsified the paint. The liquid in the glass vial would tell the truth.

Jill held her breath as John removed the

dropper from the bottle. He squirted a small amount of reagent on the orange paint of the log. She was vaguely conscious of Brent standing nearby, as though offering his silent support. For some crazy reason, she took comfort from his presence. But then she reconsidered, thinking she was imagining things. He wasn't here to help her. He was Forest Service, after all.

While John took some more measurements, Jill stared at the chemical he'd left to soak into the tree bark for about thirty seconds. Then he blotted the area with a white tissue. The smudge of residue came away bright pink in color.

"Looks good." John smiled for the first time since he'd arrived.

Jill exhaled and blinked, beyond relieved. One tree had passed the test, but what about the thousands of logs waiting to be processed through the mill? Dad had prided himself on his integrity and Alan had assured her they still ran an honest operation. She hoped that was true.

"I'm going to check a few more trees," John said.

Brent assisted, jotting measurements in a small notebook he carried in his shirt pocket.

Jill followed behind, watching helplessly as they did their work.

"Relax. This is just a preliminary investigation," Brent whispered near her ear.

She jerked her head up, the warmth of his breath tickling her cheek and making her shiver.

"It's gonna be okay," Brent added, squeezing her arm to show his support.

He flashed a generous smile and stepped away. Her gaze followed him, no matter how hard she tried to look away. She felt frozen in place. Mesmerized by his charm. She wanted to trust him. She really did. But what if he found something out of order? What if he found evidence of tree theft?

She knew the answer. He'd be compelled to take action against the mill. Alan could be held accountable. Even she could be named as a defendant. They could lose their family reputation and business. And it wouldn't matter one little bit that she liked this man and had willingly helped his sweet daughter.

Brent moved past Jill and hoped he was right. Everything would be fine. But inside, his bones were quaking. Someone had stolen that timber. It hadn't disappeared into thin air. He hoped Alan had told him the truth. That

Frank was cutting the trees late at night and driving them down off the mountain to process here at the mill.

A loud buzzing sound filled the air. Brent whirled around to look at Jill. She reached into her pocket and answered her cell phone.

"Hi, Ida." A brief pause followed as she tucked a wispy tendril of hair behind her ear. "Good. I'm so relieved. Thanks for letting me know."

She hung up and glanced at Brent.

"Frank's gotten the saws working again," she said.

Good. That news made Brent happy, too. A sudden surge of compassion flooded his chest. Jill must be so worried right now. And that made him worry, too. Because he cared about this woman. Because he liked her. A lot. Okay, maybe more than a lot. Maybe too much. He wished he dared ask her out. To be alone with her for a while. To hold her hand and talk about something besides Evie and the mill's problems.

He didn't want this business to go under. He wanted nothing but good for Jill and her family. But he couldn't analyze his feelings too closely right now. Her mom could barely stand the sight of him. He could have no future with Jill.

Forcing himself to concentrate on work, he helped John take several more samples. Each one checked out okay and he couldn't help returning Jill's pleased smile. He knew the stakes were high. Across the nation, sawmills were struggling financially. One huge ponderosa pine tree could be worth more than five thousand dollars. That money would go a long way toward paying a house mortgage or college tuition for a mill employee's kids. It was so tempting to steal trees. Brent just hoped they could find proof to convict Frank and exonerate Alan.

At the live deck, the loud whine of the head rig band saw proved that Frank had gotten production rolling again. As the sharp blades cut full logs into flitches, the air smelled of sour sawdust and burnt wood. At the planer, several men wearing hard hats, leather gloves, heavy boots and a variety of blue coveralls stood beneath an open-air canopy along the conveyer belt. The trim saws droned on in an endless cacophony of noise. Working fast, the men pulled the freshly cut lumber, sorting and stacking it onto carts according to the dimensions of the green boards.

Jill studied the workers with eagle eyes. Brent knew she must be hoping they'd make their quota today, in spite of the saws being out of commission for several hours. Between answering John's questions and Frank's belligerence, Jill had her hands full. And once again, Brent found himself wishing he could take this burden from her. That he could protect her somehow.

A tense hour later, John slid the reagent vial back into his pocket and tilted his head. "I think I've got what I need for today. Thank you for your cooperation, Miss Russell."

Jill nodded, her face pale. The engine of a forklift almost hid her shuddering sigh. She folded her arms, trying to appear passive. John didn't seem to notice, but Brent knew her too well. The way she ducked her head, then shot John a quick glance to see his expression. Her calm voice with just a bit of tremor as she took a breath. She was scared, and Brent couldn't blame her. But she was doing an admirable job of hiding her nervousness.

She accompanied him and John back to the graveled parking lot. John said goodbye and climbed into Brent's Forest Service truck. Brent held back, showing a friendly smile.

"I'm sorry we had to put you through this, Jill," he said.

"Yeah, I know." She folded her arms and shrugged, looking tense and upset.

Brent knew Jill cared about Evie. A lot. And

because of her good work with his daughter, he'd lowered his guard. He'd come to admire and respect this woman. Being near her helped him forget the pain of Lina's death. But he mustn't forget what was at stake. Jill's brother's life. Her family's business. Evie's well-being.

His own heart.

Brent mustn't forget again. It'd be best to keep Jill at a distance. To keep her work with Evie impersonal. To forget about dating the pretty special-education teacher and concentrate on his ranger job and his daughter's needs.

Maybe it was already too late. Maybe…

No! He couldn't afford to think that way.

"See you later."

"Yeah, later."

Brent climbed into the driver's seat of his truck. His forehead drew together in a troubled frown. He didn't like this any more than Jill did. He had no hidden agenda and took no special delight in hurting Alan or the sawmill. The last thing he wanted was to cut off the mill's timber harvest contracts. That would shut down the mill and put a lot of good people out of work. But if he and John McLaughlin found evidence to convict Jill's brother of timber theft, that's what he'd be forced to do.

He was the forest ranger and had a job to do. He just didn't want to hurt Jill in the process.

He started the ignition and put the truck in Reverse. Lifting a hand, he waved at Jill. She stood where he'd left her, standing in front of the door to her office. She nodded in acknowledgment, looking lost and forlorn. Worried. And he didn't like that. No, not at all.

He fought off the impulse to turn around and comfort her. To tell her everything would be okay. To keep her safe.

"I don't like this." Brent glanced at John.

Gravel crackled beneath the tires of his truck as he pulled out of the mill yard.

"I know. I can tell you like that lady. She's nice enough. Do you think she suspects what we were really doing here today?" John clicked on his seat belt and rested his right arm along the edge of the window seal.

Looking in the rearview mirror, Brent saw Jill go inside, disappearing from view. And he realized he missed her already.

"I doubt it. I think she's pretty trusting of people. I doubt she knows our investigation today was mostly for show. To make Frank think we suspect Alan instead of him," Brent said.

"Do you think Alan has told Jill about

Frank's midnight logging and processing stolen timber at the mill?"

"No. I think she would have said something if she knew. Alan's doing exactly what he's been instructed to do by keeping his mouth shut and waiting on us." Brent shook his head and gripped the steering wheel with both hands.

Jill had such an authentic openness to her. If she knew about Frank's thievery, she would have indicated it somehow. A look, a glance. The truth would be written on her face. Her personal integrity was too straightforward to keep something that important a secret. Brent didn't know how he knew that about Jill, but he did.

"She has a right to know the truth. I think we can trust her," Brent said.

"You know we can't tell her. Not yet, anyway. Not until we have proof. It'd jeopardize our case against Frank. It's the deal the US Attorney's office made with Alan."

"Yeah, I know. But I don't like it," Brent admitted.

He'd been as honest as possible with Jill and told her the LEO would be coming in this week for a preliminary investigation. And yet, he felt as if he'd betrayed her somehow. As if this was his fault. After she'd agreed to help with Evie and even defended him to her mom, he thought the least he owed her was the truth. That Alan was helping them with their investigation.

John pointed across the road. "That would be a great place to set up a surveillance camera."

Brent glanced that way and nodded. "Yeah, that would work. We can come over later tonight, after the mill's shut down."

Directly across from the sawmill, the river skirted the road, edged by thick stands of cottonwoods and willows. It also happened to be city property. An ideal location with lots of cover to hide a camera while they filmed logging trucks coming in and out of the mill late at night.

"Why don't you take me up on the mountain and show me the theft site now? I'd also like to see the cutblock where the mill's currently harvesting timber."

Nodding his acquiescence, Brent headed out of town. They had just enough time to view the cutblock before he had to return home and pick up Evie. He thought about taking her to her lessons with Jill tomorrow. And thinking about seeing the woman again filled him with both anticipation and dread. Because he wanted to see Jill, almost as much as he needed air to breathe.

Chapter Eight

The next day, Jill tossed her purse on the kitchen counter in Mom's house and kicked off her high heels. As she padded across the blue linoleum in her bare feet, she peeled off her jacket and placed it across the back of a chair. She circled around to the living room.

"Alan! Where are you?" she called to the house.

She longed to exchange her business suit for a pair of comfy blue jeans and sweatshirt, but that would have to wait. Her visit to the bank manager that afternoon had chilled her to the core.

In spite of being cold, she swiped at beads of perspiration at the back of her neck. Shock, fear and dread waged a battle inside her mind. She hoped Alan was here and not up on the mountain working. Mom had told her she'd be going over to the church to help gather gently used clothing to donate to the homeless shelter in Boise. Glad to have her mother busy in some project besides sitting around the house moping all day, Jill had contributed a couple of blouses for the worthwhile cause. Maybe she'd be able to talk to Alan in private before Mom came home and found out how upset she was.

"Hey, what's up?" He emerged from the bathroom, combing his damp hair. An eruption of steam burst from the open doorway, telling her he'd just taken a shower.

She met his uncertain smile. "Did you just get off work?"

He nodded. "Yeah, I'm home early tonight. Going out with some friends. What did you need?"

She glanced at his clean blue jeans and red polo shirt. Because of his grimy work at the mill, he showered every night. But she caught the whiff of spicy cologne and wondered vaguely if he was meeting a girl instead of his buddies from the mill.

"We need to talk, before Mom gets home." She did an about-face and gestured for him to follow her to the living room.

"Okay." He sounded easygoing, his tenor voice so much like Dad's.

Sitting on the sofa, she curled her bare legs

beneath her and tugged the hem of her skirt down over her knees. Reaching for a tasseled pillow she hugged it close against her chest. Anchoring her arms around something solid helped settle her nerves while she waited for him to join her.

He sat opposite her, adding a few final strokes to tidy his hair. "So, what's up?"

"I just paid a visit to Clarence Baker."

He shot her a quick glance. "You mean the bank manager?"

"Of course, the bank manager. Do you know any other Clarence Baker in town?"

She didn't mean to sound so sharp, but after what she'd been told, she was feeling rather grumpy right now.

Alan licked his lips and tossed the comb onto the coffee table. "I wish you'd told me beforehand that you were going to visit Clarence."

She tossed him an accusing glare. "Oh, I'll bet you do. Imagine my surprise when he informed me that it was Dad that took out the two-million-dollar loan. Not you. Why did you let me believe it was you that had buried the sawmill in debt?"

He sat back and stretched his long legs out straight in front of him before crossing his ankles. "I love Dad. He worked hard all his life and had a good reputation in this town. He would have given anyone the shirt off his back. Including the forest ranger. If the mill goes under, I'd rather have people think it was me that caused its downfall, not Dad."

His words softened her like nothing else could. She relaxed her stern expression just a bit. "But this is me you're talking to, Allie. I can't help you if I don't know the truth. I deserve that much up front. I shouldn't have to find out from the bank manager."

He sat forward and met her eyes. "I know, Jill. But maybe you can see it from my perspective. I'm your kid brother. I've always looked up to you. Admired you. Tried to make you proud. And now, the mill is failing. Because of me."

"No! I don't believe that at all." She thrust the pillow aside, wishing she could show the same calm reasoning with her brother that she exhibited with Evie. But somehow, the situations felt different. She was good at dealing with children. But issues involving the sawmill made her overly emotional.

Alan lifted a hand to quiet her. "I didn't mean to keep anything from you. I just didn't tell you that Dad had taken out the loan instead of me. Regardless, it doesn't change anything.

We've got to keep the mill going. The last thing I want to do is cast blame on someone."

She sat back and clamped her mouth shut, thinking over his words. "Yes, you're right. But no more keeping things from me, okay? If you know something, you need to tell me. If we can't trust each other, I don't know who we can trust."

He frowned and twin furrows marred his forehead. He looked away, no longer meeting her eyes. As though he were troubled by something. And once more, she got the impression he was still keeping something from her.

"Alan, is there something else I need to know?"

He shook his head, his jaw tight. "No, sis. Stop worrying. I'm doing what I'm supposed to do. Everything's gonna be fine. I know it will."

"Okay, but we're still missing five hundred thousand dollars. You're sure you don't know what Dad might have done with the money?"

He made a googly expression with his eyes. "I have no idea. Are you sure Ida's math is correct? It's possible she simply forgot to make a journal entry."

Not likely, but it was possible. "That's too much money to miss in a journal entry. There should be receipts to track back to the source. I've gone over the books numerous times. I can see where the money was received from the bank, but then it was withdrawn from the account by Dad. No receipts or ledgers show what happened to the funds. It's as though it just disappeared."

A laugh slipped from his throat. "I didn't take it, I can assure you of that. If I had, I'd be driving a whole lot better vehicle than my beat-up old truck."

She chuckled at his humor. "I'm sure it'll come to light sooner or later. I'll check again. And there's one more issue."

"What's that?"

"Frank Casewell." She released an exasperated breath and shook her head. "Remind me again why you hired that guy. He's lazy and disrespectful. Not at all good for our mill." She couldn't prevent a note of disgust from entering her voice as she quickly told him what had happened when Brent and the LEO had arrived at the mill, demanding a tour.

"I'm sorry you had to take care of that without me, but I agree," he said. "Frank won't be with us much longer, but I don't want you to say or do anything about him, understand? You stick to the office and let me take care of Frank in my own time. Trust me on this. I've got the situation under control." He met her eyes in a solemn stare and she heard the firmness in his tone. Surprising, considering he usually deferred to her judgment in such matters. But not this time.

"It's kind of hard to stick to the office when Frank won't help out and you're not around. I had no choice but to accompany Brent and the LEO."

"I'm sorry, sis. I wish I'd been there to give them the tour, but you handled it fine. Just give me a little more time to resolve the issue. Don't say or do anything about this problem. Leave Frank to me." Again, his gaze locked with hers in a persistent look filled with iron will.

Something was wrong. She could feel it in her bones. A feeling of trepidation swept over her, a nervous tickle at the nape of her neck. But she couldn't ask for Alan's trust and not return the same consideration to him.

"Okay. I'll leave Frank to you," she promised.

He flashed a wide smile, slapped his hands down on the armrests of his chair, and pushed himself into a standing position. "Hey, you going to church with us on Sunday?"

She jerked her head up in surprise. "I hadn't really thought about it. Why?"

He lifted one shoulder. "You haven't gone with us since you've been home these past two weeks and everyone's been asking about you and how you're doing."

"Tell them I'm fine."

"They'd like to see you. Why don't you come with Mom and me?"

She snorted. "The last thing I want is to stand in a circle surrounded by old friends as they quiz me about my cheating husband."

He made a tsking sound of empathy. "I think they care about you more than that, sweetheart."

Jill wasn't so certain. And yet, maybe church wouldn't be a bad idea. She'd been thinking more about God lately, and didn't feel as angry at Him anymore. Brent and her work with Evie had softened her heart more than she realized. She'd hoped she could cure Evie, but she hadn't counted on the girl and her father helping *her* heal, too.

"I'll think about it," Jill said.

"Great. I'm going out now. I'll see you later."

She swung her legs over the side of the couch and placed her bare feet on the floor. "What about dinner?"

He reached for the doorknob, giving it a quick twist before opening the portal wide. "I won't be joining you tonight. Tell Mom not to wait up."

And he was gone.

* * *

On Friday evening, Brent was running late to drop Evie off at Jill's place. As usual, he parked down the street, away from Arline's house. He suspected she preferred it that way. So the neighbors wouldn't see his truck in front of her house.

Opening Evie's door, he helped her click off the seat belt and hop down onto the sidewalk. After reaching for her dry-erase board, she held his hand as they walked to the house. In the front yard, Brent caught sight of Jill kneeling in the front flower bed. Dressed in knee-length capris and tennis shoes, and a pair of leather gloves. With her head down, she didn't see them past the wide brim of her floppy straw hat.

Snip. Snip.

Using a pair of clippers, she pruned dead branches off the rosebush.

"Ouch!" She jerked her hand back and tugged off the glove. She pressed her finger to her mouth, easing the bite from a thorn.

Her gaze lifted and she blinked in surprise. And then she gave them a dazzling smile. "Brent! Evie! I didn't know you were here."

She crawled out from beneath the bush and stood before removing the hat and sailing it onto the grass. She glanced at her wristwatch.

"Is it time for our lesson already? I must have lost track of time."

Evie gazed back with serene curiosity, her eyes filled with the light of wonderment. Brent felt her fingers tighten around his own and knew she liked being here.

In a rush of energy, Jill gathered up her bucket and clippers. "Don't worry. I'll be ready for our lesson in just a few moments."

"It's okay. No hurry," Brent reassured her.

"Evie!"

They simultaneously turned toward the house. Arline stood on the doorstep, waving to the girl.

Evie hesitated and that was when Brent realized she was never fully at ease. Not even here.

"It's okay, Evie. You can go with Mom. She has a special treat for you. I'll come inside in just a few minutes." Jill spoke in a gentle voice.

The girl gave a slight lift of her chin, almost as if Jill's approval was all she needed to know she was safe. That she could do this and it would be okay.

Evie ran to the house. Brent wasn't certain, but he got the impression she was trying to be brave. To overcome her fears of the unknown. And that brought a hard lump to his throat. Because he knew this wasn't easy for her. And next to Jill, he thought she was one of the most courageous people he knew.

Watching her go, Jill spoke low for Brent's ears alone. "Oh, yes. She's doing lots better."

He faced her, noticing an endearing smudge of dirt along her chin. "Yes, she is."

"Have you noticed more improvements at home?"

"Yes, she's now communicating with Mrs. Crawford with the dry-erase board and even helping fold the laundry."

"That's great."

He glanced at the flower bed. "My wife loved roses. Our house in Oregon was edged by dozens of red rosebushes."

Jill smiled. "Roses are beautiful and fragrant. They're easy to love. But they also have thorns. I don't know what I'd do if I had to prune dozens of them. No matter how careful I am, I always get scratched." She held up her arms to show him several thin abrasions marring her smooth flesh.

He cringed. "Ouch. You need to put a salve on those. It's too bad something so lovely can also cause so much pain."

"Yes, it is, but I don't really mind. I love working in the yard. Mom's always glad when I'm home to do the work outside. Dad always did it before. She doesn't like it much."

"I always enjoyed it, too," he confided. "Though my wife loved roses, I was the one that did the upkeep, just like your dad. About the only thing she did was cut the flowers to put in a vase on our kitchen table."

"Jill!"

They both whirled toward the corner at the back of the house where Alan stood waving at her.

"David's on the phone," he called.

Jill frowned, then murmured an apology. "Excuse me for a few minutes, please. I'll be right back."

She walked toward the door in a slow trudge, her shoulders hunched in dejection. A subtle indication she didn't want to take the call. Whoever David was, Brent had no doubt she didn't want to speak with him.

While he waited, Brent studied her work on the rosebush. Hmm. Might as well make himself useful. He picked up the clippers and continued pruning the plant. Minutes passed as he trimmed off dead stems, finding enjoyment in the task. He'd be able to finish the chore and save Jill from being injured again.

Memories rushed through his mind as he recalled doing this task for Lina. That seemed a lifetime ago. Like Arline, Brent's wife had hated working outdoors. But he'd loved it. One more thing he had in common with Jill.

"You don't need to do that."

He flinched, scraping his hand against an angry thorn. He stood and gave a nervous chuckle. "I didn't know you were back."

Jill indicated the roses, a gentle smile curving her lips. "You don't need to do my work for me."

"I don't mind. I used to prune the roses for my wife, to protect her from the nasty thorns."

She laughed. "In that case, you can prune them all you want. There's a price to pay for this beauty, isn't there?"

He stared at her lovely face. "Yes, there sure is. Who is David?"

Her smile dropped like a stone. He shouldn't have asked. It wasn't his business, but he really wanted to know.

"My ex-husband. He's looking for an old picture of his mother. It must have gotten mixed up in my things so I told him I'd mail it to him." She looked away, the happy moment evaporating like morning dew on rose petals.

"I think I heard from Mrs. Crawford that you were married once." And why did he feel glad that she was now single? He wasn't happy for her sadness, but he liked that she wasn't attached to another man. Although, since he had no plans for asking her out, it didn't make sense. Or did it?

"Yes, but it seemed my husband liked dating other women more than he liked being married to me," she said.

"You mean he cheated on you?"

"Yes. Many times." Her voice cracked and so did his heart.

"I'm sorry, Jill." And he meant it. He understood loss, but so did she. A divorce and the death of her father couldn't have been easy on her.

"It's okay. It's time I moved on." She looked down at her arm where the angry red scratches marred her alabaster skin.

"You know, I think love is a lot like rosebushes," he said.

She lifted her brows. "How so?"

"Love is beautiful. It's absolutely wonderful. But when you lose someone you care about, it hurts like a thorn ripping through your heart."

She nodded in agreement. "Very true. That's a great analogy."

Now, what had made him say that? He was being overly sentimental today. He bit down on his tongue, feeling like a heel. Her heart had been broken, just like his. Her pain tore him up inside. He couldn't imagine being this woman's husband and stepping out on her.

Obviously her ex hadn't appreciated the beautiful prize he'd been married to. If Jill were Brent's wife, he'd love and cherish her. He'd never forget he was the luckiest man on earth.

He reached out and brushed the dirt off her chin. A spontaneous gesture he didn't think to stop until it was too late. "I'm sorry. I shouldn't have asked such personal questions. I didn't mean to dredge up bad memories."

She drew away and he took one step back. A warning signal chimed inside his head, but he wanted to ignore it.

She tilted her head, looking up at him. The sadness in her eyes tore at him. He wanted to comfort her somehow. To make her happy. To see her smile and laugh.

"It doesn't matter anymore. I'm free of him now. And he can date whomever he likes, as long as it isn't me." She gave a breezy laugh, but he could tell she was hurt.

"We have a lot in common," he murmured.

She arched one brow.

"We've both lost someone we cared about. We've both been hurt before." Except that he and Lina had been in love when she'd died. And Lina hadn't betrayed him the way Jill's husband had done to her.

She nodded, her voice soft. "I can't imagine how difficult it must have been for you to lose your wife."

"Yeah, but it's been hardest on Evie, I think."

"But how *you* coped?"

He licked his lips, wondering if it was a good idea to confide so much to this woman. She was way too easy to talk to. Every time he was around her, he found himself liking her even more. "Honestly?"

She nodded, her expression eager and sympathetic.

"The Lord. I couldn't do it without Him. Every day is so difficult, but I feel God in my life. He's never deserted me, even in my darkest moments."

She looked away, and something about her demeanor told him she didn't feel the same way.

"You don't believe in God?" he asked.

She reached down and picked up her discarded gloves, tucking them inside the bucket. "I used to. But lately, I haven't really wanted to talk to Him about anything. Especially the divorce. I feel guilty, angry and sad all at the same time. I don't know how He can help me get over that."

"I know what you mean." He smiled down at her, stepping closer.

"You do?" A tear slipped down her cheek.

He gave her forearm a gentle squeeze. "Yes, I do. When you're hurt, you don't want to talk to anyone. You want to hide out and be left alone. But I've learned that's when we need to talk to God the most."

"Yes, I…I suppose you're right. But it's still hard."

"I know. And I can't tell you how much I wish…" He couldn't finish his sentence and his voice faded.

He felt mesmerized. Drawn near to her like a gravitational pull. Her sorrow reached out and slowly reeled him in like a fish on a line.

He kissed her. Gently. A soft caress as he breathed deeply of her floral scent. All coherent thought abandoned his dazed brain. All that mattered right now was Jill. Her needs and desires. Her hopes and dreams. He longed to make them all come true.

She lifted a hand and placed her palm against his chest, just over his heart. It was beating so hard at that moment, he wondered if she could feel its rhythm beneath her fingertips.

She shifted her body closer, returning his kiss. Breathing him in. But then, she pushed him away.

"Brent, I can't. Someone might see us." A

shuddering breath trembled over her as she cast a quick glance toward the house.

His thoughts whirled, like a typhoon circling in his mind. What was he thinking? He'd kissed her right in her front yard, for all the world to see.

Feeling guilty, he glanced over his shoulder, his gaze scanning the street. If any of the neighbors saw, they'd report it to Arline. And Brent didn't want to cause Jill any more trouble.

Relieved not to see someone peering at them, he turned back to Jill. "I'm sorry about that. I don't know what came over me. It won't happen again."

At least, he hoped not. He must have experienced a moment of insanity. Definitely a serious lapse in judgment. But in spite of all they both had to lose, he wanted nothing more than to pull her back into his arms and hold her close against his heart.

She turned away, hurrying toward the house. "We won't speak about it again. We'll forget it ever happened."

Yeah, right. Like that was going to happen.

He stood frozen in place. Watching her go. Longing to call her back, but knowing he couldn't do that. Not if he truly wanted to keep her safe.

Instead, he returned to his truck where he sat with the window down to catch the cooling breeze, trying to sort his muddled thoughts. He waited for an hour, every moment a torture.

What a fool he'd been. He shouldn't have kissed her, because now he only wanted more. And he couldn't have it. He couldn't have Jill. Of all the women in this town, she was off-limits. Taboo. Because of who she was, and who he was, and all the complications in-between.

So why did it have to be her that made his heart sing?

Precisely an hour later, Jill walked Evie out to the street curb. The moment he saw them, Brent sat up straight, his senses on high alert.

Jill waited on the sidewalk while he got out to greet his daughter. He opened Evie's door and helped her climb into her seat before buckling her in. When he turned around, Jill was gone. He felt deflated and empty, not being able to say goodbye. But maybe that was for the best.

Brent walked around to the driver's seat and got into the truck.

"Did you have fun with Jill?" he asked his daughter.

Evie quickly wrote the word *yes* on her erase board, smiling wide for added emphasis.

"Good. I'm glad." As he started up the engine, he couldn't help feeling as though he'd really messed up this time. He'd be lucky if Jill even spoke to him again.

What had he done? What was he thinking by kissing Jill Russell? He didn't want to do anything that might jeopardize Evie getting better. He wouldn't blame Jill if she told him not to bring his daughter over anymore. They could never be anything more than friends. He knew that better than anyone.

So why couldn't he stop wishing for more?

Chapter Nine

The following Monday, Brent returned Evie to Jill's apartment above the garage. Standing at the top of the stairs, he knocked on the door and wondered what Jill's reception might be. He waited beside his daughter. The door opened and Jill gave them her normal welcoming smile.

"What do you have there?" she asked Evie.

The girl lifted her hands, a shy smile creasing her porcelain face.

"Since you love roses, Evie wanted to give you one, to say thank you for everything you've done to help her," Brent supplied.

Jill pressed a hand against her chest and went down on one knee, looking Evie in the eyes. "Really? You brought a rosebush for me? How thoughtful of you."

Evie nodded and handed the plant over to

Jill. Then the girl quickly scrawled some words on her dry-erase board: *Dad said*.

Jill read the brief communication. "Your dad told you to bring the rose?"

Evie nodded and wrote some more: *My choice*.

"Ah," Jill said. "You picked the rosebush out."

Another brisk nod.

Jill studied the plant. It didn't look like a rosebush, but rather several sticks of cane that had been lopped off at the top. But once it was planted, the bush would start to grow.

"It's a hybrid tea rose," Brent said. "By summer's end, its petals should be pink and fragrant. And the thorns are small and soft. Not the thick, heavy thorns that'll slice through your arm."

Jill chuckled and glanced up at him. "That's reassuring. Some of my mom's rosebushes could cut through you like a machete."

She stood, holding the rosebush in one hand and taking hold of Evie's hand with the other.

"Instead of sitting outside in your truck, why don't you come inside to wait?" she asked him.

He blinked, stunned by the invitation. After he'd overstepped the bounds of propriety, he thought he'd be an even worse pariah than before.

He glanced over his shoulder, almost feeling

Arline's steel-eyed glare against the back of his neck. "You sure that's a good idea?"

She shrugged. "It'll be more comfortable than waiting out in your truck for an hour, especially in this hot weather we've been having." With her head bent, she peered askance at him. "I've got the newspaper and some magazines you can read while you wait. It'll be fine, as long as you agree not to interfere with my teaching while you're here."

That sounded easy enough. And he silently admitted he was curious about her techniques. Besides, sitting for an hour in the stuffy truck wasn't as appealing as reclining in a comfortable chair.

Without waiting for his response, Jill led Evie inside. Brent stared at the open door, wondering if he dared place his feet across the threshold. If Arline walked in and found him here, the ramifications might be harsh. But maybe not. The woman had already accepted him bringing Evie here several times per week and would undoubtedly avoid Jill's apartment until lessons were over with.

Jill pointed toward a quiet corner of the room where a soft recliner and pile of magazines awaited him. Without acknowledging him further, she sat at the table with Evie and went to work.

Stepping across the room, Brent made himself comfortable. A glass of iced lemonade sat on a coaster on the coffee table. He looked up, wondering if Jill had put it there for him. She glanced his way and nodded. Averting her eyes, he reached for the glass and almost drained it in three swallows. Once again, Jill's consideration surprised him.

As he flipped through a *Field & Stream* magazine, he made a pretense of reading. He couldn't help being curious and he listened to Jill's mild voice as she began Evie's program.

"Let's read a story first, okay?" Jill handed Evie a small children's book.

Evie opened it and Jill began to read about a little lost dog that was lonely for home. Brent watched Jill's soft lips move as she spoke, his thoughts straying to the day he'd kissed her outside in the afternoon sunshine. She'd tasted like peaches and cinnamon and he craved more of the same.

"Evie, can you point to the word *home*?" Jill asked.

Evie lifted her hand and pointed. Brent inwardly shook his head and looked away, telling himself it wasn't right for him to covet his daughter's teacher. They were both single, but he felt mildly disloyal to Lina. Because he wanted to love and marry again. But that desire would do him no good now. Not when there was no hope of a lasting relationship with Jill.

"That's right. Now point to the word *lost.*" Her voice reached him across the room, wrapping around him like a warm downy blanket.

Again, Evie did as asked.

"Yes! Very good." Jill hugged the girl, leaving one arm wrapped comfortingly around the child. And Brent noticed that Evie didn't push her away, like she did most people. Rather, she cuddled close against Jill's side.

"Now can you tell me what happened when the dog finally found his home?" Jill asked.

Evie studied the book, her brow crinkled in concentration as she scanned the words on the page.

"As soon as you know the answer, write it on your erase board," Jill instructed.

After a few moments, Evie picked up the marker and jotted something on the board. Brent couldn't help noticing her lack of hesitancy. As though she knew what was expected and was comfortable in complying.

"That's right," Jill exclaimed. "The doggie was so tired that he fell fast asleep. You're doing so well today. I believe you're already reading and writing at a third-grade level.

You're very advanced for your age. I'm so proud of you."

Stunned by this news, Brent lifted his head and stared across the room. A blaze of gratitude swept over him like wildfire across the mountain. At least there wasn't anything wrong with Evie's brain. Intellectually, the girl had already surpassed her classmates. But socially, they had more work to do. Evie needed to be able to play and interact with her friends. For that, Brent liked the display of physical affection Jill showered upon his daughter. In the past, Evie's doctors and specialists weren't affectionate with her. They acted more like automatons. Given the doctor and patient relationship, he figured that was appropriate. But bringing Evie to this home environment provided a more cozy setting. As her daddy, Brent realized Evie needed love as much as she needed anything else. And he owed all of this progress to Jill and the powers of Heaven.

Next, the girls started their writing lessons. He couldn't see what Evie wrote on her blue-lined paper, but it must have been good, because Jill praised Evie again and again.

After ten minutes, they moved on to artwork. With the patience of Job, Jill helped Evie slip on an apron and tied it in the back.

Then Jill laid out a variety of watercolors and brushes for the child.

Evie leaned over the table and rested her chin on her folded arms.

Jill lifted her brows. "You don't want to color today?"

Evie shook her head, gazing at a distant spot near the door.

"You know we have to color today, but I'll make it easy on you. Why don't you draw something that tells me how you're feeling inside?" Jill suggested.

Evie blinked several times. Finally, she sat back and studied the squares of paint. She looked up at Jill, her eyes squinting in a frown. When Jill didn't seem to notice, the girl reached for her dry-erase board and scribbled something there before showing it to Jill.

Jill shook her head, but sounded optimistic. "No, I'm sorry. You've used up all my black paint. But you can use the other colors today."

Evie released a shuddering breath. For a moment, Brent thought she might refuse. But then she picked up the brush, dabbed it tentatively in the color yellow and went to work. In studious concentration, she chewed her bottom lip. While she painted, Jill tidied the piles of books. After a few minutes, she peered over Evie's shoulder at the girl's progress.

"That's beautiful work, Evie. Would you like to show your dad?"

Evie nodded, picked up the heavy, absorbent paper, and displayed it for Brent's view. A big, yellow sun with round eyes and a nose. And the significance of the artwork brought a hard lump of emotion to Brent's throat. He gave a laughing croak of pleasure. She'd graduated from black, angry scribbles to happy, yellow sunshine. If he wasn't seeing it with his own eyes, he wouldn't believe it.

"That's beautiful, honey. We can hang it on the fridge at home," he suggested.

She nodded and whirled around to lay the painting back on the table. Her elbow clipped the paint set and the palette clattered to the floor. A splatter of wet colors smeared across the table, chair and green linoleum.

"Evie!" Startled, Brent shot up out of his seat.

The girl flushed red as a new fire engine. Before he could tell her it was all right, she ducked her head in shame and released a groan of despair. She dropped the painting and skittered across the room and darted behind the sofa. The painting sank to the floor.

Oh, no. Brent leaned over the back of the couch and saw his child squeezed back into the farthest corner, her knees pulled tight against her chest, her face buried in her hands. She rocked back and forth, little pathetic movements that told him she'd retreated into her own world. From past experience, he knew this was Evie's way of avoiding confrontation. Of hiding. Just like she'd done the night her mother was killed.

At least this time, she wasn't screaming.

"She hid behind the cashier's counter," he whispered to Jill.

She nodded her understanding but didn't speak. She gave Brent a stern look and pointed at his chair, silently insisting he sit back down. Brent remembered her warning that he could wait inside, as long as he didn't interfere with her teaching. He hadn't verbally agreed, but by coming inside and sitting down, he'd given his silent acquiescence.

He sat down, his heart plummeting. The fear of failure twisted inside his gut. He figured he'd just learned a huge lesson in how not to respond toward his daughter. But he'd been surprised. Taken off guard. When the paint had spilled, he'd overreacted. He just hoped he hadn't reversed all the progress Evie had made over the past few weeks.

Undeterred, Jill picked up Evie's painting and set it on the table where it wouldn't be ruined. She then left the scattered paints where they lay and got down on her hands and knees. While she shimmied back behind the couch, Brent considered going over to clean up the mess.

No, he better not. Without Jill's permission, he didn't dare breathe too loud or even move a muscle. And that's when he realized he trusted Jill completely. Somehow, he knew she'd make this right again. And that made him feel even worse. Because he couldn't tell her how hard he was trying to make her brother's situation better at the sawmill. He wanted to help her and Alan. To get the theft issue resolved and ease some of the tension Arline felt toward him.

Unable to keep from spying, he angled his chin so he could peer around the corner at the girls. Without asking consent, Jill scooped Evie into her arms. But Evie refused to move her hands away from her face. Cocooned behind the couch, Jill held the girl in the dark shadows.

"There, Evie. I'm not angry. Everything's okay. It's just a little spilled paint. No harm done. It can easily be fixed," Jill murmured against the girl's hair.

Brent expected Jill to pull the child out from behind the couch or leave her there to fume. That's what her other teachers had done.

Which he knew would set Evie to screaming. But Jill didn't move. She just held Evie quietly, resting her chin against the girl's forehead. Waiting. Comforting. Offering reassurance. And then Jill started to sing. A soft lullaby Brent had never heard before. Her lilting voice sounded gentle and sweet. Kind and soothing.

For a good fifteen minutes, they all sat like that. Mannequins, unable to move. Just like the day when they'd met at the gas station.

Brent felt lulled by Jill's voice, his body relaxing as he almost drifted off to sleep. She brushed her hand against Evie's hair, until the girl lowered hcr hands enough that she could peep out at the woman before quickly clenching her eyes shut again. A few more minutes, and Evie's hands lowered so they only covered her mouth. Gradually, Jill wooed the child into looking up and meeting her eyes.

"You know what? I'm hungry," Jill said softly. "How would you like to help me clean up the spilled paint? Then we can go visit Arline. I know she's made a fresh batch of snickerdoodles, just for you. Would you like that?"

Evie's lips quivered. She blinked her big baby blues and finally nodded, but she still didn't move.

Jill took the girl's hands as she slid out from behind the couch. Evie followed. With a bit of coaxing, the woman got the child to help pick up the paintbrushes while she sopped up the drying paint with a damp cloth. Brent watched in stunned amazement. It was like witnessing a miracle. He compared this moment to the day Evie was born. Something unique and wonderful. Something he'd never forget.

And when they finally left him there so Evie could go to Arline's house for her cookies, Brent still sat frozen in his seat. He rested his hands on his knees and stared at the closed door. Jill wasn't Annie Sullivan, and Evie wasn't Helen Keller, but Brent knew he'd witnessed something amazing. A tremendous breakthrough. A marvelous gift from God.

Evie had just survived what she undoubtedly perceived as a catastrophe. And she'd done it without tears. Without shrieks of anguish, and without pain.

Thirty minutes later, Jill returned to her apartment to tell Brent that Evie was ready to leave. She handed him a napkin with two snickerdoodles folded inside.

"These are for you. Evie's in the house with Mom, but she should be ready to go in a few minutes," Jill told Brent.

He stood and accepted the cookies with a wry smile. "There's no arsenic in these, is there?"

She laughed, amused by his candor. "Of course not. Mom would never deliberately poison you."

She wanted to be angry at this man, but she couldn't. Not after what she'd just been through with Evie. After all, she'd seen the angst written across Brent's face. The fear in his eyes. He'd been devastated by Evie's actions. It wasn't his fault. In fact, she was impressed by his tireless devotion to his daughter. She knew of parents who would have given up and had their child institutionalized by now. But not Brent. And she liked that about him. A lot.

He considered the speckles of cinnamon on the crinkled cookies. "I'm sorry about what happened earlier. I overreacted."

"I know. But it's not your fault. You haven't been trained in how to react. Next time, if there isn't blood gushing from somewhere, or the house is on fire, you just act like it's no big deal. After all, it's nothing that can't be fixed. And right now, Evie needs to learn that it's okay for her to make an error. That no one's perfect, and no one's going to die if the paint is spilled on the floor. Evie's been through that before, and people were killed because of a bad situation. She needs to believe that won't happen every time she makes a mistake. You understand what I'm saying?"

He nodded, his eyes registering comprehension. "I think so. For Evie, when something as simple as paint being spilled happens, she fears for her life."

"That's right. Literally. For Evie, it's not just a matter of cleaning up a mess. In her mind, the stakes are life and death. When she makes a mistake, she actually fears she might be killed."

Oh, wow! He braced the palm of his hand against his forehead, a deep breath whooshing from his lungs. "Of course. How could I be so stupid? I never thought of it that way before. I didn't realize. Oh, my poor little girl."

"Well, now you know, and that can help change how you react with her. And when she starts school in the fall, you should point this out to her teachers as well. I'm sure it would help how they treat her in the future."

He looked at her, his eyes crinkled in astonishment. "Thank you for your insight. But I still don't know how you did that."

"Did what?"

"You got Evie to come out from behind the couch and help clean up the paint."

She tilted her head. "I take it that's unusual, too?"

He raked his fingers through his short hair, his hand visibly trembling. "Oh, yes. In the past, an incident like that normally takes Evie several days to recover her composure. Now I understand why. She thought she might be killed. But you got her to respond in a matter of minutes. Just like that day at the gas station."

Yes, she had. And Jill had no idea why. She only knew she loved Evie. She genuinely wanted to help rescue the little girl from the cruel memories that must still be haunting her mind.

"We really are making progress, then." Jill couldn't prevent a smile of satisfaction from curving her lips.

"You have a gift," Brent said.

Hmm, Jill wasn't sure about that. When Evie had hidden behind the couch, she'd wondered what to do. How to help the girl. Acting on instinct, she'd decided Evie shouldn't be alone in her anguish. The child needed to know someone was there for her. That she was safe. That she could trust Jill not to yell and scream at her for making a silly mistake.

Brent stepped close, his angular face softening. "Jill, I don't want to pretend anymore. There's something going on between us that I don't fully understand."

She met his eyes, knowing he was right, but

wanting to deny it anyway. "I don't know what you mean."

"Yes, you do." He whispered the words, so softly that she almost didn't hear.

He didn't touch her, but she wished he would. His gentle consideration drew her in like a magnet. She liked being near this man, though she'd only admit that to herself.

"You're an answer to my prayers," Brent said.

Jill froze, her feet feeling as though they were nailed to the floor. His words took her off guard and left her feeling oddly emotional. She wanted to weep for what Evie and her father had been through. To hold them both close against her heart and protect them from ever being hurt again. "I've never been anyone's answer to a prayer before."

A hoarse laugh emitted from his throat. "Well, you are to mine. And I wish you could be so much more."

His confession startled her. Mostly because it mirrored her own feelings. An odd mixture of satisfaction and confusion bludgeoned her mind. Jill could hardly believe his revelation. Since her divorce, trust was difficult for her. She could sympathize with Evie in that regard. But being near Brent and working with his daughter had helped restore her self-worth.

To realize she still had a lot to offer the world. To think that maybe, just maybe, she might be able to love and be loved again.

"I can't tell you how badly I wish you weren't a forest ranger," she said.

He tilted his head in confusion, gazing at her lips. "That's a rather odd thing to say right now, don't you think?"

She laughed and took a step back. "Yes, it is."

"You'll make a great mother one day," Brent continued.

She jerked her head up and stared at him in awe. "You think so?"

He stepped closer. "Yes, I do."

She felt drawn to him. Transfixed by this kind man she couldn't quite accept. She loved Evie like her own child. The girl's success meant a great deal to her and she couldn't help wishing she were Evie's mother. And that made her realize she also cared a great deal for Brent. If only they'd met under different circumstances. If only he wasn't the forest ranger and she had no affiliation with the sawmill.

If only she wasn't going back to Boise in a few weeks.

He touched her cheek, the rough pad of his fingers brushing against her flesh. Warm, gentle and addictive. A muzzy sensation fogged her brain. With him standing so close, she couldn't think straight. All the biases and social strictures between them evaporated. She couldn't think of anything except being near him.

"Is there no way we can get past what I do for a living? Is there no way for you to simply see me as a man?" he whispered.

She almost snorted. Right now, she couldn't think about anything else except how masculine he was and how much she wanted him. Currents of electricity buzzed between them. An unseen power that was becoming more and more difficult to fight. But that was just what she must do. Fight it. Ignore it. Make it go away.

"I wish I could offer you some hope, but it would never work between us."

He nodded. "I know. Your family."

He looked away, a forlorn expression creasing his features. She wished she could be more to this man and his little girl than just Evie's teacher. But she loved her family too much to betray them by romancing the forest ranger.

"I'm afraid our relationship must remain purely professional," she insisted, her mind filled with doubts.

He wanted to kiss her again. She could see it in his eyes. The way he leaned toward her, his gaze lowering to her lips. She wanted it, too. A revelation that both surprised and frightened her. After the divorce, she'd written off men. For good. Or so she'd thought. But here she was, fantasizing about the one man that was completely off-limits to her. The only man she thought might be worth her time.

Thinking about kissing him sent her heart racing. She longed to feel the warmth of his arms around her. His strength. His confidence and compassion. The tender look in Brent's eyes didn't help the issue. In fact, it made matters worse. When she was with Brent and Evie, she forgot about her pain and started thinking that maybe she could have a second chance at love.

No! That line of thought was like a dousing from a bucket of icy water. She couldn't pursue this man. It would only alienate her family and leave her with another broken heart.

To put some distance between them, she stepped around the table. Barriers were good, both physical and emotional. Right now, she couldn't trust herself to come any closer to him.

He leaned a shoulder against the doorjamb, his tall frame silhouetted by sunlight.

"I'm sorry about this, Jill. I don't know why it has to be so hard. I wish things were different between us." He gave a tentative smile, his eyes sparkling, drawing her in again.

She wished things could be different, too. But maybe she was jinxed. Doomed to never have a normal relationship with another man. David had ruined her. He'd stolen her innocence and trust. It was just her poor fortune that she'd met another man she could possibly love and admire, and he was the local ranger. A man her family abhorred. A man the mill employees avoided like a plague of death. She couldn't see any way around the problem and it'd be best not to pursue him.

A pounding outside made her flinch. Brent stepped onto the top of the landing.

"I'll be right there, sweetheart." He waved a hand, then looked over at Jill.

In his eyes, she saw a flash of compassion and regret. Then it was gone. So quick that she thought she must have imagined it.

"It's Evie. She's waiting for me to take her home." He spoke quietly, as though lost in his own thoughts.

Folding her arms, Jill gave him a half smile. "Then, you better not keep her waiting. You should go out and celebrate tonight. Tell her how proud you are of her."

"Why don't you come with us?" he asked.

She hesitated, wanting to accept, but knowing that wouldn't be common sense. "You know why." She reached for Evie's sun drawing, handing it over to him. "Be sure to hang it on your refrigerator and tell her how much you love it."

"I will." He took the painting, his eyes darkening to a cobalt-blue. "Thanks again, Jill. You're the best."

She watched as he turned and disappeared from view. His hollow footsteps echoed as he descended the stairs. Outside, she heard him greet Evie, his deep voice vibrating on the air. After a few moments, she caught the subtle sound of car doors slamming and then the engine of Brent's truck firing up. As the sounds faded away, she felt a dizzy numbness stinging her entire body. She cared for this man. And that thought left her feeling strangely miserable and empty inside.

Chapter Ten

Over the next few weeks, Jill settled into a routine. In the mornings, she worked at the sawmill. Paying bills, sending out invoices, balancing the books. Then, she came home and helped Mom clean house and fix supper, and prepared her lessons for Evie. The girl responded readily but still didn't speak. More and more, Jill found herself wishing she could be a permanent part of the child's life. An enduring part of Brent's life, too. And for a few short days, she even began to think it was a possibility. To love and find happiness again. With Brent.

That dream shattered abruptly when Jill was forced to pay an unannounced visit to the Forest Service office. Standing before Brent's cluttered desk, she folded her arms, feeling angry and betrayed. The weekend had proven to be more than difficult and she couldn't believe she'd ever believed in this man.

"Hi, Jill. Have a seat." Brent welcomed her warmly, scooping a pile of papers off the chair in front of his desk.

"No, thanks. I'll stand."

He plopped the papers onto the edge of his desk before meeting her gaze. "Can I get you something? We've got soft drinks and water."

"No, I'd rather get down to business."

His forehead crinkled in confusion. "Okay. What's up?"

"I thought you were my friend and that you believed in Alan's innocence," she cried.

His mouth rounded in surprise. "I am. I do."

"Then why are your Forest Service employees stopping every one of our logging trucks to demand a log receipt?"

He sat down, the springs on his high-backed chair creaking. He took a deep breath and let it go, twining his fingers together over his flat abdomen. "Is that what's got you so worked up?"

Yes. No. She wasn't sure anymore. Right now, she was trying hard not to use her anger to cover her deep-rooted emotions for this man. She didn't want to contemplate what she was really feeling, for fear of where it might lead. Better to ignore it and just keep moving forward.

"Yes, I'm upset. Every one of our logging trucks is being stopped twice. At the top of the mountain, and at the bottom. Your Forest Service employees are pulling them over and demanding a logging receipt. The trucks are held up while everything is checked out to ensure we aren't using the same tickets more than once."

He nodded, his expression showing no shame. "Yes, it's important for us to follow through, especially when we've had a theft. This is nothing new. You know that."

"The stops aren't new, but so many of them are. It's delayed our work and forced us to use up over half of our log decks in storage. At this rate, we may run out of logs and have to shut down production."

He slanted his head and contemplated the short gray carpet for a moment. "I'm sorry for that inconvenience, but I'm happy to say all your trucks have checked out so far."

"Then you won't stop any more of our trucks?" She held her breath, awaiting his answer.

He leaned forward, resting his elbows on the top of his desk. "You know I can't promise that, Jill. Not ever. Stopping those trucks isn't personal. It's just business. I hope you can see that."

A brittle sensation settled in her bones. Fear and anger battled with rational thinking. She'd agreed to help Brent with Evie, and look how he rewarded her. By jeopardizing the mill's productivity. A part of her understood he was only doing his job. And yet, she also felt deceived. He'd never lied to her, but he'd kissed her, and she wanted more. She'd begun to hope that maybe they could...

No! This situation was exactly why she could never be with this man. Their loyalties were at opposite spectrums. She must learn to keep her distance.

"We've been doing everything we can to assist with your investigation. And I've been helping with Evie, too."

"Yes, and I appreciate every bit of it. You've been wonderful," he said.

"Then, why? Why are you doing this?"

"I'm not doing it to you, Jill. I'm just doing my job."

She stared at him, not knowing what to think. Not knowing what to believe. She only knew she was confused. About the timber theft, about him and about her place in his life.

Correction. She had no place in his life. She'd help Evie as much as she could. Then she'd return to Boise and leave Brent and his daughter on their own again. For so long, Jill had wanted to get out of Bartlett. To make something of her life. But now, something had changed inside her. Somewhere along the line, her heart had become entangled with Brent. And now that she'd recognized it, she couldn't seem to let it go.

"Fine. I understand. I just thought we were…"

"You thought we were what?" he asked in a low, husky voice.

"Better friends than this." She spoke in a rush, wishing she were anywhere but here. She couldn't reveal her inner feelings to him. Not now. Maybe never. She'd been hurt before and didn't want to feel that way again.

"We are. We're very good friends," he said.

"Then, why?"

He released a breath of frustration and raked his fingers through his hair. "Because it's my job."

She gave him a steel-eyed glare. "That sounds like a cop-out to me."

He stood and walked around the desk, reaching out a hand. "Jill, don't be like that. I'm sorry you're caught in the middle of this nasty situation. Please believe I only have you and Alan's best interests at heart. If you'll trust me a while longer, I think everything will soon come to light."

Trust him? Not in a million years. There was too much at stake. The mill. Her family's livelihood. The jobs of dozens of mill workers she cared about.

"I don't know what you're talking about. I don't understand. Not at all." Her voice vibrated with impatience.

She was dangerously near tears, and she didn't even understand why. All she knew was that her feelings for this man bordered on love. But now, she realized it was an illusion. A phantom dream she could never have.

He touched her arm, but she jerked away. His fingers scalded her skin. Not a physical burn, but a memory of how much it hurt to love someone else.

"I know this is difficult for you. I wish I could tell you more, but I can't. I'm asking for your trust," he said.

In his eyes, she saw compassion and friendship. But his actions belied his words.

She blinked up at him, her thoughts scattering, her mind numb. His cryptic words told her there was definitely more going on here than she understood. Something behind the scenes. Something bad. She could feel it in her soul. And once again, she couldn't help wondering if Alan knew more than he was saying. Was he in on this covert affair? Did he know what Brent was keeping secret from her? If he did, it seemed both men were determined not to confide in her. And after all the lies David had told, her tolerance level for clandestine exploits was nil.

Lifting her chin, she met Brent's eyes. "I've had my fill of deceit. There was a time when I gave my trust willingly. Now people have to earn that from me."

He nodded, his eyes crinkling with regret. "I understand, and I can't blame you either."

That was it? That was all he had to say to her? He understood, yet he sure wasn't willing to offer any reassurance. To tell her he'd back off of their logging trucks. That he cared for her and would never let her down. If she were honest with herself, that's what she longed to hear. And then she'd tear down the barriers between them once and for all and fling herself into his arms.

She'd admit that she loved him.

"Thanks for your time." She turned toward the door, her hands shaking.

She moved slow, giving him the opportunity to call her back. To tell her everything would be okay. But he had his own demons to fight. He'd lost his wife too soon. He probably still loved her more than anything. And Jill wished someone in this world cared for her that way.

"You're welcome. I'll see you tomorrow night, when I bring Evie over for her lesson." His voice sounded low and careful. As though he fought a silent battle within himself.

"Yeah, tomorrow night." No matter what, she couldn't turn Evie away. Not to save her life.

Yes, something definitely was going on that Jill didn't understand. But this meeting today had solidified something for her. Brent was still the forest ranger and she was the mill owner. And they could never be anything more.

With misgivings, Brent watched Jill leave his office. He longed to call her back. To confide in her. To tell her that cracking down on her mill's logging trucks was a tactic he'd been ordered by the LEI to use in order to keep Frank Casewell off guard. So the man wouldn't suspect that the Forest Service knew about his thievery. He wanted to catch a thief. But he wanted Jill, too. He felt torn between his affection for her and fulfilling the responsibilities of his job.

He felt awful. Like he'd lost his best friend. He'd thought he and Jill were drawing close enough for love and something strong and lasting. Then he'd seen the suspicion and doubt in her beautiful amber eyes. He'd heard the fear and anger in her voice and known he'd probably destroyed the little headway they'd made together.

He wished he could bring Jill into the loop. Wished he could tell her how hard he was fighting on behalf of her brother. That he was doing everything in his power to prove Alan's innocence.

After Lina's death, he'd thought he would never love again. That happily-ever-after had passed him by. Then, he'd met Jill. He loved her, he realized that now. But his profession stood between them.

He thought about the day he'd kissed her. The fragrance of her hair, the softness of her lips. The way she'd lifted her hand and rested it lightly against his chest, just over his heart. A feeling of protectiveness had filled him like the colors of a rainbow. All swirling and dancing inside. For the first time in over a year, he was happy. As though he could conquer the world.

And he could never let it happen again.

He had a job to do. He had to keep his focus on Evie and his work. Not on romance. Not on Jill.

Not on love.

He owed Jill so much. She'd done great

things with his daughter. Evie rarely cried any-more. She'd stopped having nightmares. She smiled and even laughed. Jill had done that for them. And he was determined to return the favor, by clearing Alan's name.

Brent had never met Jill's father, but he'd read the Forest Service files. Her dad had an honest reputation around town. He'd rarely got-ten into trouble for any timber violation and, if he did, it had been one of his employees that had caused the problem and he'd taken care of it immediately. But now, Alan was in charge, and he was highly inexperienced. Brent won-dered if Frank Casewell had known he could take advantage of the young man. Brent hoped Alan hadn't been in on the deal from the be-ginning. That he hadn't gotten cold feet and then decided to come to the Forest Service for help. Either way, the situation was too compli-cated for Brent to consider deepening his rela-tionship with Jill.

Maybe staying unattached and single was for the best. He didn't dare take a second chance. He didn't want to pit her against her mom and brother. Nor did he want to hurt her in any way. Not after what she'd come to mean to him. She deserved peace and happiness. She deserved a man who could love her without reservations. And he feared he couldn't give her that. Not as long as her family didn't approve of him.

Chapter Eleven

The tires on Jill's car crackled against the gravel as she pulled into the driveway at home. It'd been a busy day at work. She killed the engine and gazed at the dark house. No lights on. No one home. Alan had driven to Boise to finalize a contract with a new buyer and Mom had gone with him to do some shopping at some of the bigger stores. Alan had said they'd be home very late. Which meant dinner would come out of a can. Jill didn't mind. She had the place to herself and time to relax.

She thrust open the car door and stepped out. The fragrance of Mom's rosebushes enveloped her along with the warm night air. Dressed in a pair of calf-length skinny jeans and sandals, she stood for several moments, enjoying the summer breeze as it rustled through the old oak tree in the backyard.

Stepping into the kitchen, she kicked off her shoes and padded barefoot across the green linoleum. Opening the refrigerator door, she blinked at the bright light as she scanned the shelves for something to eat. A variety of leftovers, salad makings and fresh fruit stared back at her. She settled for cold pizza and strawberries along with a tall glass of milk. Simple and easy.

Taking her plate into the living room, she flipped on the TV to catch some evening news. She'd propped her feet up and started to relax when her gaze scooted past a picture of Dad hanging on the wall. Which reminded her that she needed to check her father's office for his tax returns. She'd searched the mill office with no success.

The thought made her groan out loud. After a hard day's work, she'd rather sit here and doze. But rifling through Dad's office would undoubtedly upset Mom. She'd better do it now, while Mom was gone.

Dropping her feet to the floor, Jill sat up. Forcing herself to stand, she trudged down the hall. The door to Dad's office was closed. Mom didn't like it disturbed, even to vacuum and dust.

Jill paused, her fingertips resting lightly on the brass knob. She hadn't been in this room since the day after Dad had died and she didn't want to go in now. This room had been his inner sanctum. Filled with memories. Whenever she'd been upset about something, she'd come here for solace. Even when she'd found out David had cheated on her, Dad had held her on his lap and wiped away her tears. He'd told her everything would be all right. That she'd recover and be happy again one day. That she was his shining star. And she'd felt better when she left him.

He'd died three months later.

If only Dad were here now. He'd know what to do about their financial woes and this trouble brewing with the Forest Service. Somehow he would make everything right.

But Dad was gone, and Jill had never felt more alone.

Taking a deep breath, she opened the door. As she peered into the dark shadows, she dug her toes into the soft carpet. It felt like her stomach was in her throat.

Taking a step, she flipped on the light and looked around. Everything appeared normal, just as it had been when Dad was still alive. Nothing out of place. She imagined she caught his familiar smell. Peppermint and sandalwood, and another scent uniquely his own.

A picture of her parents on their wedding

day sat on the desk. Mom was smiling at the camera, but Dad was gazing at Mom. With so much adoration that it almost made Jill's teeth hurt. Her parents had been so much in love. And Jill had imagined sharing that same adulation with her own husband. In all her childhood dreams, she'd never once thought she might get married and her husband would cheat on her.

Fighting off the burn of tears, she looked away. Feeling swindled and disappointed. For some reason, Brent came to mind. He was so much like Dad. Kind and attentive. Worried about his little daughter. Trying to earn a living the best way he knew how, while seeing to the needs of his family. His deep, soothing voice always brought Jill a modicum of comfort. She'd come to anticipate her teaching sessions with Evie with relish. In fact, she couldn't wait to see Brent again. And when he'd held her in his arms and kissed her that day out in Mom's flower beds, she'd felt cherished and safe. The first time she'd felt that way since Dad's passing.

"Enough of that!" She shook her head, realizing her thoughts had led her into dangerous territory. It'd be more productive to focus on the chore at hand.

Gripping the silver handle, she opened the

filing cabinet and shuffled through a raft of manila folders. She slid the door closed and it gave a metallic slam as she turned toward the rolltop desk. Pens and dusty papers lay scattered across the top, as though they hadn't been disturbed since Dad left them there. She rummaged through a stack of files, then opened a drawer. Empty. As she slid it closed, a shiny glimmer caught her eye. She jerked it back open and reached in to clasp a single key resting inside.

Turning the key on her open palm, she read the tag attached. Two simple words, scrawled in Dad's shaky handwriting: *Rainy day.*

Hmm. How odd. She cocked her head to one side, wondering at the puzzling message. What did it mean? And more importantly, what did the key open?

She closed her hand as a light clicked on inside her mind. Maybe the key opened the safe in Dad's office at the mill. It'd be so like Dad to keep them separate. In this sleepy town, robberies were quite rare. Also, the key could be obsolete. Something that used to fit a lock they no longer had.

There was only one way to find out.

Padding down the hallway, she picked up her purse, slid her shoes on and reached for the back door. She flipped on the porch light so she could see her way down the rock path leading to the driveway. The night air smelled of honeysuckle and dinner cooking next door at the neighbor's house. Jill felt a strange, comforting sensation as she got inside her car and started up the engine. As though she belonged here in Bartlett. Something she hadn't felt in many years, in spite of growing up in this house.

She switched on the headlights. Putting the car into gear, she headed outside of town. She made a left turn, the black asphalt giving way to dirt road. Within minutes, she'd driven the short distance to the sawmill. She was about to turn the car and unlock the front gate when a flash of light across the vacant road caught her eye.

Whipping her head around, she stopped her car, letting the engine idle. She squinted into the dark expanse near the river, thinking she'd imagined it.

There! She saw it again. As though a flashlight were moving among the tall cattails and willows. Maybe it was kids out late, playing along the river. Hide-and-seek was a favorite pastime. With only one restaurant in town and no movie theaters, kids had to figure out other ways to entertain themselves. Night games were a favorite.

But what were they doing down by the river at this late hour of the night? It wasn't safe. Someone could fall in and drown. It'd happened before. And she didn't like them being so close to the mill. A lighted match and the whole place could go up like a torch.

She had better check it out.

Pursing her lips together, she pulled over and parked her car along the side of the road and got out. Picking her way through the bushes, she stepped lightly, keeping the moon in her line of sight so she wouldn't lose her way. The roar of the river filled her ears just to her right. And another sound she barely recognized. A man speaking.

Deep voices reached her ears. Not the younger sounds of kids, but of fully matured adults. A few more steps and she'd be able to see them. What on earth were they doing out here at this time of night…?

She bumped into a tall man's solid torso. A strong hand closed over her wrist and she screamed. Jerking back, she prepared to fight and run.

A flash of light blinded her eyes. "Jill?"

She ducked her head and froze, blinking to clear her dazed vision. She knew that voice.

"Brent! What are you doing here?"

He lowered the beam of light. In the eerie

shadows, she saw his deep frown and narrowed eyes. He wasn't happy to see her here.

"I could ask you the same thing. What are you doing out here so late?" he growled.

Before she could respond, John McLaughlin stepped out from behind a tall cottonwood. His right hand cupped the butt of his revolver hanging from his hip. Even in the dark, she caught the angry glint in his eyes. Both men wore their uniforms, the badges pinned to their shirtfronts gleamed in the scattered moonlight. John's face looked harsh and unapproachable.

Just beyond the two men, another dark form took shape. In a quick glance, Jill took in the shadowed tripod and camera partially concealed by heavy bushes. The extended lens was pointed directly at the entrance to the sawmill.

Her mouth dropped open in outrage. "You're filming activity at the mill."

It wasn't a question. Even in the gloom, she could see the guilt written across Brent's face. She'd caught him fair and square. And a lance of anger pierced her chest.

"So this is how you show your friendship to me? By spying on my family's sawmill," she cried.

"Jill, this isn't about my relationship with you. It's about a theft investigation. It's got nothing to do with us."

"It has everything to do with us. That mill belongs to my family. It belongs to me."

"But you haven't been here. This problem occurred while you were living in Boise." His voice lowered, and she got the impression he was trying to soften the blow.

"We've cooperated every step of the way," she said. "So why are you out here late at night in this cloak and dagger stuff? I have a right to know what's going on."

He took a deep breath, then let it go. "You're right. I think it's time you knew the truth."

"You...you do?" Her shoulders tensed. Right now, she didn't know what to think.

"Yes, I do." He threw a questioning glance at John.

The LEO hesitated, then nodded reluctantly, as if he had no choice. "Okay, but keep her close until this thing is over with."

Brent tugged on her arm. "Come with me."

She folded her arms and planted her feet. "I'm not going anywhere with you. Not until you tell me what's going on."

He held out a placating hand. "If you'll come with me, I'd rather show you. My truck's parked right over there behind the bridge. I'd like to take you for a short ride. Everything will soon become clear. Please."

She peered through the shadows, unable to

deny the fierce suspicion broiling inside her gut. Warning chimes rang loudly inside her head. She wanted to know the truth, but she feared what he might show her. Alan was out of town with Mom, but she refused to believe he was culpable in the theft. "It's late and I should go home. Can't you just tell me what's going on?"

He brushed a jagged thatch of hair back from his high forehead. Even in the darkness, he couldn't hide his appeal. She felt the attraction between them like an old friend. Right now, she wanted to throw herself into his arms. But that wouldn't do her or her family any good. She hated the suspicion that had settled between them.

"Later, I'll take you home. Come on. You'll be safe with me," he said.

His words washed over her like a warm blanket. She longed to trust him. To confide her deepest fears. But what if he let her down? She'd tried to put aside her ex-husband's betrayal, but it had left a bad taste in her mouth that just wouldn't go away. Besides, Brent was a man on a mission and she doubted he'd let Evie's teacher get in the way of catching the timber thief.

Worried and a little frightened, Jill took his hand. His long, warm fingers folded over her own as he pulled her up the embankment. A man that had kissed her and made her believe happy endings were possible after all. A man she'd fallen for in spite of her vow to never love again.

"I'm parked right over here." He pointed toward the river.

His cajoling voice surrounded her. Soothing her nerves. Drawing her in. She couldn't fight him to save her life. But she didn't know what to make of this. She'd trusted David, and look what that had gotten her. Nothing but heartache. And as she trudged behind Brent, she prayed he didn't do the same.

"Where are we going?" Jill's voice sounded thin and trembly as she sat stiff and unyielding in the passenger seat.

"Be patient. It's just a short drive," Brent reassured her. He longed to tell her more, but figured it'd be best to let her see with her own eyes and judge for herself.

"What's this for?" She picked up a camera with a nightscope and high-powered zoom lens. An expensive piece of equipment.

Reaching out, he took it from her and placed it back on the padded seat between them. "You know very well what it's for."

He didn't mean to sound abrasive, but tonight would make or break his case. More than anything, he wanted to put an end to this friction between them. He wanted to prove Alan's innocence. But he hadn't expected an uninvited guest to tag along and watch everything play out before them.

She folded her arms and locked her jaw. Turning her head, she watched the dark scenery flash past her window. "I don't like this. Not one bit."

Her fear was almost palpable. It rushed at him like a living thing. And he hated it. Especially since he'd put it there. All he wanted to do was keep her safe. To protect and love her.

Yes, he loved her. He finally admitted it to himself. Ever since she'd given Evie the little dry-erase board. Such a simple, considerate gesture. But it had locked Jill into his heart and he hadn't been able to dislodge her in spite of his best efforts.

A relationship with this woman was futile. Loving her would bring both of them nothing but pain. Jill would never trust him. Especially after tonight.

A low squawk in his earpiece made him jerk. He reached up to his waist and turned the volume down. Jill's eyes followed his movements, taking in the special equipment he was wearing for the night.

"What's that for?" she asked with wide-eyed uncertainty.

"Just to keep in contact with John."

"Will he tell you what's going on?"

"Only if he needs to. I just want to help, Jill. To do what's right," he said.

She snorted, flipping her long blond hair over her shoulder. "I think you're more interested in getting a conviction than helping my family."

He longed to deny her words, but thought it was too little too late. After tonight, he'd be lucky if Jill ever spoke to him again. And that upset him more than anything. Evie had flowered under Jill's tutelage. She'd responded and grown so much over the past weeks.

So had he.

He slowed the truck and took a right turn off the black asphalt, following an abandoned dirt road. Since Jill had grown up in this area, he figured she knew exactly where she was.

"No one ever comes up here," she said.

"That's right. It's nice and lonely. A perfect route for timber thieves."

She bit her bottom lip, her eyes wide.

They skirted the edge of Cove Mountain. A few minutes more and he pulled his vehicle off the road into a sheltering copse of thick piñon-juniper trees. He killed the engine, unclicked his seat belt and reached for the camera. Removing the lens cap, he took a few pictures, to ensure the mechanism was working properly. Everything must be perfect. He might never get another chance.

Jill swiveled around in her seat, watching his movements with wary eyes. She glanced at the road, which was visible from their vantage point, yet his truck should go unnoticed by someone passing by. He'd taken a lot of time to scope out this hiding place and it was perfect.

"You're expecting someone to come along?" she asked.

He nodded. "I'm afraid so."

"It won't be Alan. He's in Boise with Mom." She spoke with firm insistence, as though trying to convince herself.

"I hope it's not Alan," he said.

She released a pensive whoosh of air. Her slender shoulders tensed, but she didn't speak. For long minutes, they sat in silence.

"Where's Evie tonight?" She whispered the words without looking at him. As though her voice might chase off anyone who happened to be driving by tonight.

"With Mrs. Crawford."

"Oh."

"I told Alan to go into Boise today. To get far away from Bartlett," he said.

She jerked a surprised glance his way. "You did?"

He nodded. "Yes, and I hope he did as I asked him to do. You shouldn't expect him home until the wee hours of the morning. I told him to take someone with him. To make sure he had several witnesses in Boise who could testify that they saw him there late at night, before he started home. I told him to not come back until there was absolutely no chance he could be involved in what you're about to see."

"Why would you do that?" She frowned in confusion.

"To ensure he has an alibi."

She took a sharp inhale. "Oh, Brent. I'm not sure I even want to know what's going on. I'm too afraid to ask."

"Then just sit back and wait. Everything will come to light soon enough." Reaching across the seat, he opened a case on the floor and reached inside. He handed her another night-scope with a zoom lens.

She took the scope and held it with both hands, staring at it as if it was a snake that might bite her. "It's heavy. What am I supposed to do with this?"

"Look through it." He nodded at the road,

not daring to take his eyes off that spot. He caught her expression out of his peripheral vision. A mixture of relief and dread.

She lifted the lens up and peered through it, her fingers twisting the focus bar. He barely heard her low whisper. "This is amazing. Even though it's pitch-black outside, I can see everything with perfect clarity."

He held the camera in his lap, ready to snap pictures at a moment's notice. Long minutes later, he heard a sound. The low drone of a big engine. It grew in intensity. Bright fog lights from a large truck flashed past them, then bathed the deserted road in eerie shadows.

Jill ducked down. "Someone's coming."

"They won't see you," he assured her. "Besides, my truck has tinted windows. They can't see us inside the cab."

She sat back up as he lifted the camera and pointed it at the road, his finger on the trigger. A huge logging truck lumbered past, driving slow across the deserted road. In the moonlight, Brent could see its back hayracks filled to capacity with logs. He pressed and held his finger down. The shutter of the camera clicked in rapid succession.

Looking through the nightscope he'd given her, Jill gasped. He didn't look her way until the truck had passed by and he'd gotten the pictures he needed.

"That was Frank Casewell driving," she said.

"That's right. And you're now a witness to what you saw."

She pressed a hand to her mouth, her face shining pale in the dark shadows. "He has no business being out here so late at night. He must be stealing timber."

Brent didn't say a word as he set the camera on the seat and pressed the call button on his earpiece. "John, this is Brent. Come in."

A brief pause followed.

"You've got a truck headed your way. Be careful," Brent said.

Another pause, then he looked over at Jill, conscious of her watching him with eagle-eyed precision. "You just warned John that Frank's on his way with a load of stolen timber."

He started the engine, flipped on the headlights, then put the truck in gear. "That's right."

"Is John going to try and make an arrest tonight?"

"Yes, John and a few other officers with him."

Her mouth dropped open as she understood the situation. "There's more than one officer hiding out at the mill."

It wasn't a question.

"Yes, Jill. We have a warrant. And I don't want you in harm's way when they make their move."

She gripped the armrest as Brent pulled the vehicle onto the dirt road. When she spoke, her voice sounded shrill with alarm. "But what if Alan didn't go to Boise? What if Mom's covering for him, Brent? What if he's here in town? What if he's at the mill?"

In that moment, Brent realized how much she'd just confided to him. Her deepest fears were written across her ashen face.

"You really think your mom would do that?"

She covered her face with her hands, her words muffled. "I don't know what to believe anymore. I hope not."

He admitted to himself that he was surprised she would confide such a thing. It was another indicator of how close they'd become. Otherwise, he wouldn't have let her accompany him tonight. But now, he doubted she'd want anything to do with him.

"Be calm. It should be over with soon now," he assured her.

She snorted. "That's easy for you to say. Your brother isn't the one that might be involved in theft."

"You think he's in on it?" He lifted a brow, hoping against hope that wasn't the case.

"No, I don't. But what if he got back into town early and went over to the mill? What if Mom's with him?" She left the sentence hanging in the air between them like a dark storm cloud.

Brent gripped the steering wheel like a lifeline. "I hope he didn't do that. I hope he followed my instructions completely."

She looked at him, her face white as a fresh sheet hanging on Mrs. Crawford's clothesline. "What are you going to do now?"

"John and the other officers are waiting for me back at the mill. I'd like to drop you off at your house before I join them."

"No, I want to stay with you." A bit of panic and desperation edged her voice.

He bit his bottom lip, thinking this over. His work tonight could get ugly and he didn't want her there to see it happen. Like always, he wanted to protect her. To keep her safe. He wanted to shield her from any horrible memories that might haunt her later on when this nasty business was over with.

He glanced at her from across the seat. Her eyes glittered with unshed tears, her face tight with determination.

"I'd rather you stayed home tonight. I promise I'll call you the minute it's done. And no matter what happens, I'll be there for you," he said.

"No, I'm not leaving and you can't make me."

Yes, he could, but he wouldn't do that. Not in a million years. He couldn't stand to hurt her that way.

He waited for her to say something more about her brother. She sat quietly twining her fingers together in her lap. She startled him with her next words. Words that told him she felt a connection between them, too, but couldn't act on it any more than he could. Not as long as this theft trouble stood between them.

"No, I'm going with you. I won't get in the way, I promise. I can face whatever happens, but I want to make sure you stay safe."

Chapter Twelve

Jill gripped the armrest with tight fingers. She waited for Brent to insist she go home, but he didn't say a word. Just nodded his head once and pressed on the gas. And she couldn't help feeling that he trusted her. Enough to let her into his world. So, why couldn't she do the same?

Maybe she should call Mom and Alan, to see where they were. Hopefully, somewhere in the vicinity of Boise.

Slipping her hand into her pocket, she pulled out her cell phone and checked the connectivity here in the mountains. The bright light in the dark cab of the truck made her blink. Only one bar. She doubted she could reach anyone right now.

She jerked when Brent reached out and closed his hand over the phone. He didn't pull it from her grasp, but he pushed it down toward her lap.

"I'm sorry, Jill. I can't let you call anyone right now. Not until we arrive at the mill and see what we're dealing with there."

Oh. She hadn't thought about that.

"I just wanted to know where Mom and Alan are and if they're okay. I wasn't trying to warn them."

He nodded. "Your family's fine. I know you're worried. So am I. But we'll have to let this play out now. No cell phones."

She sucked in a shallow breath, wondering if he'd try to take her phone away if she pressed the issue. Maybe he didn't trust her as much as she thought. She couldn't help wondering how far he was willing to go to catch this thief. But fighting over her cell phone would devastate her. Not only because she wasn't up to the animosity it might create between them, but also because she loved him. She understood how difficult this must be for him. And for her. She wanted to trust him. She really did. But so much had happened in the past to make her suspicious of men. Brent owed her nothing. He'd kissed her, but he'd never told her he loved her. They'd made no commitments. And right now, he had a job to do, and a thief to catch. Whether it involved her brother or not.

She tucked her phone into her pocket, speaking in a low voice. "I don't want to jeopardize your case, but I also don't want anyone to get hurt."

"I'm afraid it's too late for that, Jill. After tonight, someone's going to jail. We'll have to let the system do its job and trust that everything will work out for the best."

Trust. That word kept coming up between them.

Her heart gave a powerful thud. His cryptic words brought the reality of the situation into sharp, agonizing focus. Yes, someone would go to jail for this and she prayed Alan wouldn't be included.

As they drove through the night, she didn't know what to expect. She didn't like Frank, but she didn't want to see him go to prison either. No doubt he had at least one accomplice. Probably an employee from the sawmill. Which meant Jill knew them well. Maybe they were even good friends.

She didn't speak as the forest buzzed past the window in a melee of tall, dark shapes. Her stomach swirled with urgency. A shiver of fear swept down her spine. She wanted off this mountain. Wanted out of this truck. Right now.

She said a quick prayer, asking God to keep her family safe and to protect the mill from harm. The first prayer she'd uttered in many long months. In her pain and anguish over the divorce, she'd abandoned God. But now, she needed Him more than ever. And maybe inviting Him back into her life was the first step to trusting Brent.

As the town lights came into view, an anxious energy pulsed through her veins. The truck bounced as the tires traded dirt road for smooth, black asphalt. The hulking shapes of the post office and grocery store rushed past, making the dark Main Street seem even more deserted.

Brent jerked his hand up to the earpiece and she could tell he was listening.

"It's time," he said, calm and steady.

"Who's speaking to you?" Jill asked.

"John. He's moving the team into position," Brent said as he glanced her way.

"Team?"

"Yes, we've got three LEOs and five US marshals with us tonight."

A sick feeling settled over her. She never suspected a thing. Not like this. Not this big. "This is a sting operation, isn't it?"

He nodded. "I'm sorry I couldn't tell you about it earlier, but I was sworn to secrecy. We've been monitoring the night activities up on Cove Mountain and over at the sawmill for weeks now."

She understood, but still felt betrayed. It was her family's mill, after all. She tried to tell herself that she had no right to feel offended. Brent hadn't done anything wrong. He didn't owe her anything. He was just doing his job.

But it still hurt. A lot.

"Jill, I'll let you stay with me on one condition," he said.

Her face heated up like a flame thrower. She felt completely alone and at his mercy. If only she knew that Alan and Mom were safe. That they weren't involved. "And what's that?"

"That you don't leave this truck or my side until I tell you it's okay to do so. Agreed?" His penetrating eyes seemed to peer into her mind.

Jill heaved a sigh of exasperation. No doubt he'd take her home if she refused. And she'd go stir-crazy if she couldn't be here and know what was going on. But something hardened inside of her. Something she didn't dare contemplate. "Agreed. But if anyone gets hurt tonight, I'll be very upset."

He blinked at that and locked his jaw. "I understand. But no one's going to get hurt. Not if I can help it."

His promise didn't sway her. The situation was out of his control. He couldn't stop it. Like a giant boulder rolling down a mountain, anyone that stood in its path was bound to get squashed.

He made a left turn and headed toward the other side of town. They were moving faster than the heavy logging truck and they caught sight of Frank turning into the mill yard. Brent slowed his vehicle to a crawl, then pulled into the bushes along the river's edge and shut off the engine.

Jill looked over at the camera tripod, sitting right where they'd left it two hours earlier. John was nowhere to be seen, but a small green light blinked to indicate the camera was on and filming everything.

Brent nodded toward the mill and answered her unasked question. "I'm sure John's inside now."

Yes, hiding out with the rest of the team. Waiting for Frank and his accomplice.

Reaching across the seat, Brent handed her the nightscope. While he peered through the camera lens, she lifted the scope to her eyes and gasped. As Frank drove the big logging truck inside, several armed officers swarmed the front gate. From her vantage point, she caught sight of someone standing on the roof of the mill office, pointing a rifle down at the yard below. She could see the luminous words

US Marshal written clearly across the back of his jacket.

"Brent! They've got guns," she cried.

He reached across the seat and squeezed her arm. "Steady, sweetheart. They're all law enforcement. Trust that they know what they're doing. It'll be over with soon."

Trust? Someone could be killed tonight. Someone she knew and cared deeply about.

Her hands trembled as she lifted the night-scope again. Bright halogen lights flared inside the mill yard and she jerked the scope away, blinking at the sudden flash. A loud voice boomed through the air, as though coming from a megaphone.

"US Marshal Service. We've got you surrounded. Back away from the truck and put your hands in the air and no one will get hurt," the voice demanded.

Jill couldn't see what was happening inside the mill yard, but her imagination ran wild.

"What's going on? Tell me," she insisted.

"It's a raid," Brent said.

Yes, that was obvious. But who was in there? She had to know, but didn't dare open the truck door and run inside. She'd given her word to Brent that she'd stay with him. It was the most difficult promise she'd ever made in her life, but she intended to keep it.

Long minutes passed while Jill sat there trembling. Finally, Brent reached up to his earpiece and nodded.

"All clear. They're bringing them out now," Brent told her with a slight smile of satisfaction.

"Them?"

He nodded, his eyes narrowed with resolve. "Frank Casewell and two other men. He had two accomplices. We can go in now, but you must remain with me. Okay?"

She nodded, saying a silent prayer in her heart that Alan wasn't with them and no one had gotten hurt.

They climbed out of the truck. Brent took her arm, helping her pick her way across fallen tree trunks and bushes that covered the dark ground. Just as they emerged from the trees, two black sedans pulled out of the mill yard.

Jill recognized the men sitting in the backseats. She gasped and pressed a hand to her mouth. "Bill and Tommy Baker."

"You know them?" Brent placed himself in front of her, so the two men wouldn't see her in the dark shadows. A protective gesture that didn't go unnoticed by Jill.

She nodded. "Yes, I went to school with both of them. They're brothers. Friends that have worked for the mill for years. Their mom has pancreatic cancer, but no medical insurance. They're both family men with kids to feed. They've had it tough lately, but I never thought they'd resort to stealing timber."

Sitting in one car, the brothers had their shoulders hunched, as though their hands were cuffed behind their backs. They hung their heads, looking lost and so alone. Frank Casewell sat in the backseat of the second sedan, his eyes filled with belligerence as he glared his defiance at the officers.

Inside the mill yard, Jill stood back and watched with wide eyes as US marshals scurried around taking photographs and gathering evidence. Jill could only imagine what would happen to Bill and Tommy's families now that they'd been arrested. And she made a silent vow to help them through this difficulty any way she could.

John greeted Brent with a strong handshake. "The Baker brothers are singing like canaries. Cooperating all they can. They'll probably cop a deal and get a reduced sentence. But Frank Casewell isn't saying a word."

"Is there just the three of them?" Jill asked.

John's potent gaze swung her way. "Yep, that's all the arrests we'll be making tonight."

Jill released a mighty exhale, realizing she'd been holding her breath. Alan wasn't here. For now, he was safe. But she was still eager to talk with him and Mom.

"I'm glad it's over with," Brent said.

Jill was, too. And yet, a horrible feeling settled deep inside her soul. She loved Brent deeply. Had even begun to hope there might be a way for them to be together. But she didn't see how. Not now. By tomorrow morning, the small town's paper would have this story plastered across the front page. Everyone would know what had happened and the part Brent had played in the arrests. In a town filled with loggers, most people wouldn't approve of Brent even if he was in the right. Most of them would side with Bill and Tommy Baker, even if the men were guilty of timber theft.

Tonight's escapades had capped Jill's relationship with Brent in a final deathblow.

Hunching her shoulders, she slid her hands into her pockets. Her fingers closed over the key she'd found in Dad's desk earlier that evening.

"Is it okay if I go inside the office?" she asked.

"Sure. I'll tag along," Brent said.

Right now, she wanted to be alone. To check Dad's safe, then go home. But since law enforcement officers still swarmed around the place, she doubted Brent would leave her side for even one moment.

Feeling confused and discouraged, she

headed toward the office with the forest ranger following close on her heels.

X

Now that the sting operation was over with, Brent wanted to let Jill go. To let her be by herself. He sensed she needed time alone. But he couldn't do that. Not until she was away from the mill and home safe.

He stood in the moonlight, waiting for her to pull out her key and open the office door. A repetitious beep sounded and she quickly flipped on the light, punched in a code and shut off the alarm system.

"I won't be a minute. I just need to check something out." She walked to the back, unlocked the door to Alan's office, and slipped inside.

He followed, standing on the threshold, watching as she knelt on the floor before a heavy, black safe. Withdrawing a key from her pocket, she inserted it into the lock and turned. The safe gave an audible click.

Jill gave a sharp inhale, her hand resting on the knob for the count of three. Then, with a quick twist of her wrist, she pulled the door wide.

"Oh, no! You have got to be kidding me." She spoke as if to herself, pressing her hands to her mouth.

Wondering what would cause such a strong reaction, Brent stepped near enough to look inside. Tidy stacks of money lined the back wall of the safe.

"Wow!" he said.

She reached out a trembling hand to ruffle the edges of one stack of bills. Her movements seemed hesitant and startled. Disbelieving.

"You didn't know the money was in there?" he asked.

She shook her head, her voice wobbly. "No. I found the key at home tonight. No one's been in the safe since Dad died. We all thought it was empty. But Dad must have put the money here just before his death."

Her cell phone rang and she scrambled to pull it from her pocket. She hesitated, waiting for Brent's nod of approval before she flipped it open, then pressed it against her ear. "Hello? Oh, Alan! Where are you?"

She paused, listening.

"So you just got into town. And Mom's with you at home?"

Another pause.

"Oh, I'm so relieved." She quickly told her brother about the late-night raid on the mill and that Bill and Tommy Baker were involved with Frank.

"You already knew that?" she asked with incredulity, her gaze lifting to Brent. "But why didn't you tell me?"

Brent leaned against the corner of the desk, listening as her brother filled her in on his part of the sting operation. Brent felt unbelievably happy that tonight's events had gone so smoothly and that Alan had taken his advice and gone to Boise.

Jill blinked up at him, her eyes wide. "Yes, Brent is here with me now. I'm coming home. I've got something important to tell you, too."

Another pause, and then, "Okay, I'll see you in a few minutes. Stay right there. I love you, too. And give Mom a hug for me." She hung up the phone, slid it into her pocket, then gazed at Brent with accusing eyes.

"I couldn't tell you," he said before she could ask.

She nodded. "I understand. I don't like it, but I understand."

"How much money do you reckon is in the safe?" he asked, trying to distract her. Hoping she wasn't angry at him for keeping Alan's part in the investigation a secret.

"Five hundred thousand dollars," she said.

He gave a low whistle. "That much money should be in a bank."

"Yes, you're right. And first thing in the morning, I'm going to call Sheriff Newton to accompany me, and that's exactly where I'm going to put it." She slammed the door to the safe, twisted the knob, then tugged to make sure it was locked securely.

She stepped over to him, shaking her head. "Dad never trusted banks. But it'd be so easy for someone to rob this office. Especially with Frank Casewell skulking around. He had the code to the alarm system and could have easily broken into Alan's office."

"Why do you think Frank didn't try?"

"You're assuming because Frank steals timber that he'd also steal money from his employer."

Brent snorted. "Where do people draw the line? Why is it okay to cut down trees illegally, but not okay to break into a safe? I think most people are honest, but they prove it every day by obeying the laws."

She nodded. "You make a good point. I suspect Frank never tried because we all said the safe was empty. He knew we were struggling financially, so he must have believed us."

Brent agreed, but listened without judgment as she explained about the missing money and how the new equipment at the mill had taken them to the edge.

"I'm so glad we found the missing money," she admitted.

"Will this ease your financial woes?" Brent asked.

A restless laugh slipped from her throat. "Oh, yes. Beyond my wildest dreams."

"Good. I'm so glad tonight has turned out well for you." He reached out and caressed her arm, longing to pull her close. Longing to tell her how much he cared for her.

She stepped out of his reach and took a deep breath. A horrible, swelling silence followed.

"Try to take it easy on Alan," he said. "He couldn't tell you about any of this. He was trying to do the right thing when he first came to me, but the US Attorney wanted a conviction and threatened to prosecute him if he told anyone about the case until it was resolved."

"I see." Her voice sounded terse, her shoulders stiff with tension.

"Jill, I've also tried to do what was right. I hope you're not upset with me."

"No, you did your job."

"Then you're not angry at me?"

"No, why would I be angry?"

Maybe she wasn't angry, but she wasn't happy either. He knew her expressions well enough and could tell she was troubled by him.

"Jill, I never wanted to hurt you. In fact, I

want to be close to you. You see, I've fallen in love with you."

Okay, he'd done it now. Laid his heart on the chopping block. But he realized he had to take a chance. If he didn't trust her, if he didn't try, he might never know the happiness she could bring into his life.

Her mouth dropped open. "Oh, Brent. Don't say that."

He stepped closer. "But it's true."

"No, don't you see? We can never be anything more than we already are."

"Why? Just because you're a mill owner and I'm a ranger? That shouldn't get in our way. Not if we really care about each other."

He waited, hoping she would give him some sign that she felt the same way.

"But what about the next time it happens, Brent? I am a mill owner. You are the forest ranger. There will always be friction between us. Every time the Forest Service suspects a tree theft, or every time my loggers leave slash up on the mountain, or bulldoze too close to a creek, or violate the harvest boundaries, there's bound to be trouble between us."

"There doesn't have to be. Love is built on trust and mutual respect. You know I'll do my job, but I know you'll tell your employees not to break the law."

"It's not that simple."

"Yes, it is. I love you. Do you love me?"

She quirked her brows in confusion and gave a sad little laugh. "You must think I'm more easygoing and predictable than I really am. I'm not a saint, Brent. I'm a woman with a lot of faults."

"You didn't answer my question."

Did she love him? Oh, he hoped so. But the seconds ticked by and she didn't respond. His heart plummeted, but he tried to rally. To dispel her fears so she could see how good they could be together.

He took hold of her hand with both of his and lifted it to his mouth. She didn't pull away and he placed a soft kiss on her open palm, then another kiss against her forearm. "The scratches from your mom's rosebushes have healed. Remember how they gouged your arm? Those beautiful flowers we both enjoy can really hurt. It's the same with love. We open our hearts, and it feels wonderful. It's lovely to us. But it can hurt sometimes, too. Very deeply. If we don't grow the roses, we won't ever get hurt by them. But we won't have the beauty they can bring into our lives either. I've fallen in love with you, Jill. I can't say it more simply than that. I want you in my life. Forever. I can't promise there won't be difficult days, but I can promise I'll never cheat on you, and I'll never walk away. No matter your faults. No matter how hard it might get. I'll always be there for you. All you have to do is say you love me, too."

She gave a croaking laugh and withdrew her hand. He gazed into her eyes, willing her to say yes. But no matter how strong his commitment was, he couldn't force her to love him back.

"I don't know if I'm ready for this, Brent."

"Then I'll give you as much time as you need. I'll wait forever, if I have to. I told you once, you're the answer to my prayers."

"Don't say that." She backed away, shaking her head.

"It's true. You're the most generous, kind woman I've ever met. What you've done for Evie is amazing."

"We can't base our relationship on my work with Evie. I'm her teacher. I love that little girl. But loving you is a different matter entirely."

His heart gave a painful jerk. "You don't love me?"

She hesitated, not meeting his eyes. "I...I don't know what I'm feeling right now. Tonight has been very difficult for me. Right now, I just want to go home and think."

He slipped his hands into his pants pockets

and looked down at the dull, gray carpet. "I understand completely."

Yes, he did understand. She didn't want him. She didn't love him. And right now, his heart felt as though a trillion rose thorns were ripping through it like a machete.

He lifted a hand toward the door. "Come on. I'll walk you out to your car."

He didn't touch her as she turned and headed in that direction. He wanted to, but realized that would only deepen his anguish. And right now, he needed to put some distance between them. So he could forget the deeply personal feelings he'd just confided to her.

He waited while she reset the alarm, shut off the lights and locked the front door. Then he walked out into the yard. John and the other officers were still mopping up the crime scene. It'd be a long night for them. But it was time for Brent to collect Evie and go home.

He accompanied Jill to her car. The rush of the river nearby filled his ears. He opened the door and waited for Jill to slide into the driver's seat. She'd buckled her seat belt and started the ignition before he closed the door.

She rolled down the automatic window. "Thank you."

He tilted his head, confused by her words.

After all, he'd given her a rather emotional night. "For what?"

"For your honesty. I know this hasn't been easy on you either. I appreciate what you've done for Alan."

But it wasn't enough. Not for them.

"You're welcome."

She put the car in gear and pulled away. He stood watching her back taillights fade from view. More than anything, he longed to get into his truck and follow her home. To pull her into his arms and find a way to make her love him. To figure out a way to overcome the obstacles standing between them.

He didn't move. Not for a very long time. Finally, with a heavy heart, he climbed into his truck and drove the dark streets to Mrs. Crawford's house. The sprinkler system whooshed across the green lawns, the crisp night air smelling of lilacs and damp cement.

He knocked quietly. The elderly lady answered after a moment, wearing a red bathrobe, her gray hair filled with pink foam curlers.

Evie lay sprawled across the sofa, a soft quilt over her as she slept. She seemed so relaxed. So calm and serene. He owed Jill and Velma Crawford an awful lot.

"Did your late work at the office go okay?" Velma asked with a sleepy smile.

He'd told her he was working late, but hadn't confided about the sting operation. She assumed he was working at the Forest Service office, which was fine. By tomorrow morning, he had no doubt she'd find out the truth. He figured Bill and Tommy Baker's wives would be called in to the police station. They'd try to post bail, and word would soon spread.

"Everything went fine." He scooped Evie into his arms before carrying her out into the warm summer night.

The girl blinked her eyes and curled against him, but she didn't speak. And he realized no matter how much time passed, he longed to hear her call him Daddy again. Just one word. That's all he asked. But she didn't say a thing.

As he drove them home, he couldn't help feeling like an integral part of their life was missing. Jill should be here with them. He knew it in the depths of his heart. An abiding conviction that she was the one for him. The only woman he could envision himself loving ever again.

He just wished Jill believed it, too.

Chapter Thirteen

Jill sat at the kitchen table with her mom and Alan, having lunch. She felt despondent and lost. Two days had passed and Brent hadn't called. Nor had he brought Evie over for her lessons the night before. Jill hadn't really expected him to, but she couldn't help feeling disappointed just the same. She missed them both. More than she could say. They'd wormed their way into her heart and she'd grown accustomed to being with them. More than she had imagined.

Now she had nothing to keep her in town any longer. The mill was back on track, and the end of the summer was whisper-close. Time for her to return to Boise and her solitary life. But somehow, it wouldn't be the same without Brent and Evie, and her family nearby. She never would have believed it, but she knew she'd miss Bartlett, too. The neighborly comforts she found in this small town. A place filled with memories, both good and sad.

Returning to Boise wasn't all bad. She still had a job she loved, working with special-needs kids.

So why was she miserable at the prospect? Oh, she didn't need to ask why. His name was Brent Knowles. And she loved him so dearly. But she loved her family, too. And they would never approve of her being with the ranger.

She picked at her tuna fish sandwich, missing Brent and Evie like crazy. Telling herself she'd get over them in time. Wishing she dared call Brent to ask how Evie was doing.

Just to hear Brent's voice.

"What do you think, Jill?"

"Hmm?" She looked up at her brother. Both he and Mom stared at her with a bit of exasperation. She hadn't been listening.

"Did you see yesterday's newspaper? We made the front page." Alan stuck the town paper in front of her nose. All nine pages of it.

"Actually, I've tried to avoid it." But yes, Jill had read it several times. Her gaze scanned the article again, which mentioned how Alan had worked with the authorities to catch the real thieves.

Mom stood and crowded close, looping her

arm over Alan's shoulders as she peered at a picture of Frank handcuffed and standing in front of the mill office, just as he was being carted away by John McLaughlin and several US marshals.

"That Frank was such an awful man," Mom said. "I'm glad he's not working for us anymore."

Jill handed the paper back to Alan. "Frank had help, you know. He didn't do this alone. I hope our next mill manager is an honest man."

Alan flashed a wide grin, slathering mayo on a piece of bread as he made another sandwich. "He will be, since it's gonna be me. After Dad died, I didn't feel confident in my work, so I hired Frank. But I think I know what I'm doing now."

Jill chuckled. "Yes, I agree. The mill is in good hands now."

"Have you been over to visit Shelley and Carma Baker, yet?" Mom asked.

Shelley and Carma were the wives of Bill and Tommy Baker. They had nine children between the two of them, not to mention an ailing mother to care for.

Jill nodded. "Alan and I went to visit them earlier this morning. They're doing well, all things considered."

Alan chuckled and took a bite of his sandwich. He chewed for a moment, then swallowed. "They were understandably upset, until we posted bail and assured them their husbands could have their old jobs back at the mill. As long as they both promise not to pull something like this again. Tommy and Bill are hard workers and I want to give them a second chance, but I won't tolerate theft ever again. We're gonna run a clean operation, just like Dad used to do."

Wow! This situation had changed Alan somehow. Gone was the adolescent young man who didn't seem to know quite what was going on. Alan had really grown up over the summer. Maturing. Becoming the strong man Jill always knew he could be.

Mom pursed her lips with approval. "I'm glad, son. Enough people have been hurt by this. It's time to move on now. I think your father would approve."

Jill gazed at her mother with surprise. "You seem very forgiving."

"Well, it wouldn't do to kick the Baker brothers while they're already down. Not if they're willing to make amends. It'll be hard for them to pay the fines, but everyone deserves a second chance."

Jill leaned her elbow on the table and rested her chin against one hand. A flare of hope ignited inside of her. "Does that apply to the forest ranger, too?"

How she wished her mom could forgive Brent for any perceptions of wrongdoing. How she wished her family didn't dislike him so much.

"Hmm." Mom gave a disapproving growl, an expression of dislike firmly written across her face.

"You know, Brent's been generous to me when he didn't have to be. He went out of his way to help us," Alan said.

Bravo, Alan! Jill wanted to kiss her brother, but didn't dare cause a scene that might send Mom to her room for the rest of the day. Nice try, anyway. Mom's expression of distaste didn't change one bit. After all, Alan still hadn't been cleared of any wrongdoing. Not yet. Which caused them all a bit of nervousness. He'd told Jill last night that he'd waited almost two months before going to see Brent, to tell the ranger that the mill was being used to process stolen lumber and that Frank had threatened to burn the place down if Alan warned the authorities. The US Attorney's office could take that as partial guilt. The authorities still could show up on their doorstep to arrest Alan. Which left Jill and Brent nowhere. And yet, deep inside, she knew if she left town without telling Brent how she really felt about him, she'd regret it for the rest of her life.

She faced her mother, choosing her words carefully. "Mom, Brent's a good man. I wish you could…"

The doorbell rang.

"Oh! I wonder who that could be." Mom bustled to the front of the house without a backward glance.

Jill lifted her gaze to Alan. He leaned against the kitchen counter and contemplated her with a mixture of compassion and sadness, but he didn't say a word. No doubt he felt the same about Brent as Mom did.

"Evie! Oh, it's so good to see you, sweetheart." Mom's voice filtered into the kitchen.

Jill shot out of her seat and raced into the living room. One thought pulsed through her brain. If Evie was here, then Brent must have brought her. And Jill had to see him again. Even if it was the last time. She had to gaze upon his beloved face at least one more time.

Dressed in his crisp Forest Service uniform, he stood inside the doorway with his daughter. The moment she saw him, Jill screeched to a halt. His gaze riveted on her and she couldn't help smiling. She felt suddenly deliriously happy and sad all at the same time.

"Hi, Jill." He gave her an endearing lop-sided grin.

"Hi, there."

"Brent, what's up?" Alan came into the room, slinging his thumbs through his belt loops.

"I've got some news for all of you." Brent stood behind Evie, resting his hands on her slender shoulders. The girl brushed a sun-kissed wisp of hair out of her eyes and smiled wide, showing a gap where a new tooth was starting to grow in front.

"Oh! What is it?" Mom shifted nervously beside her son.

"I'm glad you're all here together," Brent said. "Evie and I are just on our way up to Cove Mountain. I'm planning to review a new cutblock of timber for your loggers to harvest. I thought I'd stop by and bring you the news."

Mom folded her arms, her face tense but not exactly hostile.

"That's great. Our mill can get back to work, then. We appreciate that." Alan cleared his voice. "I know it's still a bit early yet, but is there any news on my standing with the US Attorney's office?"

Brent met the other man's eyes with kindness. "As a matter of fact, Frank has finally confessed to everything. He burned down a mill in Missoula a few years ago, and he even confessed to that."

"And Bill and Tommy Baker?" Arline asked.

"They've been released on bail. They'll have some hearings to face and possibly some steep fines to pay, but they won't spend any more time in jail. Now it's up to them to keep their records clean."

"Good, we can help them get back on track," Alan said.

Brent reached a hand toward Arline. The woman stepped back, watching him with misgivings. "Mrs. Russell, I know how it feels to worry about someone you love, and I wanted to come over here and tell you this next news myself. Because of Alan's help, the US Attorney's office has cleared him of any wrongdoing. He's free."

Mom gasped. So did Jill.

"Really?" Arline said.

Brent nodded. "Really."

"Oh, son. I'm so happy." The woman hugged Alan and brushed at her damp eyes.

Jill hugged her brother, meeting Brent's eyes over Alan's shoulder. She could see the truth written on Brent's face. She knew he wouldn't say such a thing if it wasn't true. And that's when she realized she trusted this man. With complete faith, just as she trusted the Lord.

"Well, we better get going. We're on our way up to Cove Mountain," Brent said their destination again.

He turned to go, but Mom tugged on the sleeve of his Forest Service shirt. "Thank you, Ranger."

Brent inclined his head. "You're most welcome, Mrs. Russell."

He stepped out onto the front porch with Evie. Jill followed them, hugging her arms around herself. In spite of the waves of hot sunlight, she felt suddenly cold. She didn't want them to leave. Not when it meant she might never see them again.

"Thank you, Brent. I appreciate you coming over here today." She spoke the words in a shallow rasp, her heart breaking in two. At least they were parting on a happy note. But it wasn't enough for Jill. Not anymore.

He turned and studied her face for several heart-pounding moments. Then, he reached up and brushed his fingertips against her cheek. His touch sent a zing of awareness through her. She wanted to throw herself into his arms and stay there forever.

"If you ever need me, you know where to find me. All you have to do is call and I'll be there for you," he said.

His words sank deep into her soul, but it was

too late. After the night of the raid when she'd rebuffed his confession of love, she couldn't blame him for being hurt. If only Mom could let this go. If only her brother wouldn't disapprove. Jill's family meant everything to her. Since she was a little girl, she'd dreamed of bringing her own children here to this house one day, to visit their grandma. And being with Brent would undoubtedly create unwanted contention within the family.

One word from Alan and Mom was all Jill needed. One word that they could be friends with Brent, and Jill would cancel her teaching contract in Boise. She'd stay right here in Bartlett with Brent and Evie forevermore.

But those words didn't come as Mom and Alan went back inside the house.

Taking Evie's hand, Brent walked down the sidewalk. Evie broke free, holding back. The girl took Jill's hand, standing close against her side. Evie's face puckered in an obstinate grimace. She didn't want to go.

Brent turned, looking at his daughter with expectancy. When he spoke, his voice sounded gentle but insistent. "Come on, honey. We can't stay. We've got to go now."

Evie shook her head. "Stay."

Jill froze. What was that? She couldn't move. Couldn't breathe. No, it wasn't real. She hadn't heard right. Evie hadn't spoken. Had she? It'd been too faint. A small whisper. A figment of Jill's imagination. Maybe it was the wind. Or the sound of a car passing by on the street.

Brent took a faltering step, his face drained of color. He tilted his head to one side, as if struggling with the same confusion. "What did you say?"

"Stay." Evie spoke again, a little louder this time.

Brent's eyes widened and his mouth dropped open. He looked stunned. A hoarse, emotional laugh slid from his throat and he came to kneel just in front of his daughter.

"Evie, you spoke," Jill cried.

The girl pressed her face against Jill's abdomen, her words muffled but still intelligible. "Stay here with Jill."

In a stupor of delight, Jill knelt down and pulled the child into her arms for a tight hug. "Say it again, Evie. Say anything."

"Jill. Stay with you," the girl spoke against Jill's neck.

"Evie! Oh, Evie!" Brent enfolded the two of them with his strong arms. His deep laughter mingled with exhales of sobbing joy. A celebration of success.

Jill's gaze locked with Brent's. His eyes mirrored her absolute joy. After more than a year of silence, the child that had been lost to him had finally returned.

"Oh, sweetheart. I love you so much," he murmured over and over again as he spread kisses across her face.

Tears ran down his cheeks. Jill couldn't stop crying either. This seemed too much like a miracle to them. Something amazing and impossible and wonderful.

Finally, Brent pulled back and the three of them gazed at each other with tremulous smiles.

"You know we'll always be the best of friends," Jill told Evie. "Nothing will ever change that. And we'll see each other again."

"Promise?" the girl asked.

Jill gave a shuddering laugh. It was so good to hear Evie's sweet voice. "Oh, yes, darling. I promise."

Evie gave a sad nod, her eyes filled with a maturity too advanced for her tender years. She knew Jill was going away and that they'd only see each other when Jill came home for visits. None of them could hide the truth of the situation from this intelligent child.

"I love you, Evie." Jill hugged Evie again, breathing in the child's warm, fruity shampoo.

"I love you," Evie whispered back.

The commotion must have brought Mom

and Alan to the door, because they stood there and smiled. Sharing in this amazing and joyous occasion.

They each laughed and wept together, but it couldn't hold back the passage of time. Finally, Brent took Evie's hand and brushed wisps of blond hair back from her face. "Come on, sweetie. Time for us to go."

Evie didn't fight him as he tugged her along, but she stared over her shoulder at Jill.

Tears scalded Jill's eyes, and she couldn't keep them from falling. Down her cheeks they plummeted unheeded. But what did her smudged mascara matter when her whole world was walking away from her?

Jill waved goodbye, her heart bursting into a trillion shards of broken glass. She watched in misery as the love of her life and his precious daughter got into the Forest Service truck and drove away.

An arm slid around her trembling shoulders and she thought it was Alan. But no, it was Mom.

"You should go after him," Arline whispered.

Jill jerked her head to look at her mother with startled wonder. "What?"

"You heard me right. I said you should go after him. He's a nice man and you don't want to lose him." Arline showed a serene smile of acceptance.

Alan stood beside them and nodded. "For sure. I'd take the ranger for my brother-in-law over that rotten ex-husband of yours any day of the week. At least the ranger's an honest man. We can trust him."

Jill gave a choking laugh, glancing between the two of them. Her family. And how she loved them. But not in a million years had she expected this turn of events. "Do you both mean that? Really, truly?"

"I do," Alan said. "You know, there's no reason for you to go back to Boise. Ed Sallinger has a sweet little daughter with Down's syndrome. And Terry Bates has a son with autism. And of course, there's also Evie. I'm sure there are other special-needs kids in the area that we don't even know about. You can continue your work right here in Bartlett. Why don't you stay?"

Jill hadn't thought about that, but Alan was right. She could stay right here where she felt most at home. She didn't need to live in Boise to perform the work she loved. And then she could be near Brent and Evie, too.

Mom pressed her palms against Jill's back. "Go after him. He and his daughter make you happy. I can see that. And life's too short to let love pass you by. I never thought I'd say this, but he's the first reasonable forest ranger I've ever met. And he loves you, too, that's obvious. If he's what you want, I won't stand in your way. And if Evie is any indication of the grandchildren you two might give to me, then I'm fine with that, too."

"Oh, Mom!" Jill whirled around and hugged her mother, overwhelmed by the myriad of emotions flittering through her chest. She felt as though she was finally free. As though a leaden weight had slid off her shoulders.

Alan dangled her purse and car keys in front of her nose. "If you're gonna go chasing after the ranger, you better put on some shoes first."

He glanced pointedly at her bare feet.

Mom chuckled. "I never could keep shoes on you, even when you were a little girl."

Jill laughed. "I love you both."

She grabbed the purse and keys and raced through the house to the backyard. Taking the steps up to her apartment two at a time, she jerked on a pair of socks and tied her tennis shoes. Armed with her family's approval, she scurried outside to her car. One thought pounded her brain. Brent and Evie. She had to find them. Right now. She had to tell them that she loved them. That she wanted to be with them always. That she never wanted to be parted from them again.

High on Cove Mountain, Brent viewed the pristine beauty of the alpine meadow and tried to jot memos in his notebook. The cutblock would include ponderosa pine and some Douglas fir. If the loggers got started, they could finish the harvest before the weather got too cold. Then the Forest Service could start a replanting program up here in the spring…

His hand shook, making scribbles of his notes. He had to draw a line through the words and start again. Now, what had he been writing? He couldn't remember. His thoughts were still back in town with Jill. All he could think about was leaving her. Maybe never seeing her again.

A chilling melancholy overshadowed his heart. He couldn't work today. If he had to beg on his hands and knees, he was going back to Arline's house to ask for her daughter's hand in marriage.

He clicked off the pen and slipped it into his front shirt pocket as he looked up at Evie. Oblivious to the pain and chaos he was harboring, she stood in the middle of the meadow, blissfully picking white and yellow wildflowers.

Humming. Some little tune he'd never heard before. A chorus of angels couldn't have sounded more heavenly to his ears.

He smiled, his body relaxing. His pulse rate slowed. He couldn't remember the last time he'd heard his child sing. Now she was talking again, it was as if a dam had broken inside of her. She'd chattered nonstop on the ride up here. And if Evie could start speaking again, then surely he could convince Arline Russell to let him marry Jill.

He sent a prayer heavenward, knowing the Lord could make it happen. He just had to have faith. Some way. Somehow. He had to convince Arline and Alan that he was the man for Jill. That he could make her happy...

"Hi, there."

He whirled around and dropped the notebook in the dirt. Jill stood before him, wearing her calf-length skinny jeans and tennis shoes. Her warm blond hair hung about her shoulders in soft curls. He could imagine the silky texture and longed to bury his face in it and breathe in her delicate fragrance.

He blinked, trying to clear his mind. "Are you a mirage?"

She shook her head and stepped close, a gentle smile curving her perfectly beautiful lips. "No, I'm real."

Above the meadow, Evie's voice rose in crescendo. She didn't know Jill was here yet.

Jill gestured toward the child. "She's happy again."

"Yes. But wh...what are you doing here?" he asked.

"I came for you." She took another step that brought her close enough to touch his chest.

As she lifted a hand and rested her palm directly over his heart, he took a sharp inhale. He didn't dare speak, for fear she might disappear.

"I had a heart-to-heart talk with my family," she said.

"You did?" He quirked his brows, his mind filled with hopeful wonder as he reached up and covered her hand with his.

"Yes, and they told me I should come after you. They've given me their blessing to be here."

"They...they did?" Oh, he felt stupid and tongue-tied right now. All rational thought fled his dazed brain.

"Yes, so I've come here to tell you that I'm in love with you."

A hard lump settled in his stomach. "You are?"

She nodded. "Yes, I am."

His throat felt like dry sandpaper. He couldn't speak. Couldn't move a muscle. He was completely at her mercy, and he prayed she soon put him out of his misery.

"I love you and Evie so much," she said. "I want nothing more than for us to be together as a real family."

And then, she did something that tore his heart in two and sent his spirit rocketing to the sun. She took his hand and knelt on one knee. Looking up at him with adoration gleaming in her eyes, she cleared her throat.

"Brent Knowles, I love you more than anything in this world. Please marry me. Because I want to be happy for the rest of eternity."

He whisked her up into his arms, swinging her feet clear of the earth. Holding her tight to his chest, his voice rasped against her cheek. "Oh, darling. Don't you get on your knees. Not before me. Not ever. That's my job. I love you, too. So very much. And yes, I'll marry you. As soon as we possibly can."

"Really?" She laughed, as though she couldn't believe it was true.

Finally, he set her on her feet. "Yes, really. I never thought this was possible. I thought because I'd threatened Alan and the mill that you'd hate me forever."

She gazed up at him with adoration. "No, you did your job. You did what was right. Even Mom and Alan realize that. And what you've done has made me respect and love you all the more."

Standing close, he cupped her face with his hand, hardly able to believe his dream was coming true. "That day you rescued Evie, I had no idea you'd also be rescuing me."

"And I had no idea you'd be rescuing me." She breathed the words on a sigh. "I think Evie will make the cutest flower girl the world has ever seen."

"I have no doubt she'll like knowing you're about to become her new mommy," he conceded.

"God has blessed us so generously." She spoke in awe, as though she still couldn't believe their happiness was coming true.

"He has indeed." Pulling her into his arms, Brent kissed her deeply. He breathed her in, knowing they'd found their rose among the thorns. And after all, what more could they ask for?

* * * * *

Dear Reader,

Having grown up in small towns throughout the Western United States, I actually worked in a sawmill once. You might find it hard to believe, but there weren't a lot of jobs available in my town for a kid seeking employment. At the age of fifteen, I spent one summer pulling boards off the green chain, to pay for my school clothes in the fall.

The crime of timber theft is personally a very important one. Timber theft is a billion-dollars-a-year crime. Stealing timber destroys ecological and watershed systems, and takes something precious from future generations of people.

I must point out that the Forest Service would plant seedlings in March, when the ground is nice and damp, not in May and June when the weather is turning hot. Additionally, they never would start planting seedlings in a theft area until after law enforcement had completed their investigation. I have violated a few of these rules in order to make this story work. I hope you'll forgive any inaccuracies and focus more on the overall message I'm trying to convey. That love can conquer fear and pain. That even when we feel abandoned, God walks with us through every trial of our faith. Just as Evie needed rescuing from the silent world she'd built around herself, so too did Brent and Jill need rescuing from the hurt they'd experienced in their lives. And the atonement of Jesus Christ is the ultimate rescue for each of us.

I hope you enjoy reading *The Forest Ranger's Rescue*, and I invite you to visit my website at leighbale.com to learn more about my books.

May you find peace in the Lord's words!

Leigh Bale

LARGER-PRINT BOOKS!

GET 2 FREE
LARGER-PRINT NOVELS
PLUS 2 FREE
MYSTERY GIFTS

Love Inspired®
SUSPENSE
RIVETING INSPIRATIONAL ROMANCE

Larger-print novels are now available...